ROSY'S RECYCLING TEA SHOP

Rosemary Blake

ebook ISBN 978-1-9162554-4-9
paperback ISBN 978-1-9162554-5-6

Cover design by: Gabriella Regina https://grbookcovers.com

Author website: www.rosemaryblake.co.uk

CONTENTS

ROSY'S RECYCLING

TEA SHOP

CHAPTER 1

'No don't go in.' Rosy's mother burst out of the church, her hands clenched into fists.

Rosy faltered. She felt her father's arm tense, clamping her to him, but she was still stepping forward focusing on reaching the church doors. The headdress pulled on her hair roots as Tanya, holding the veil, failed to keep up. Rosy broke free from her father's grasp and charged towards the entrance.

'No stop.' Her mother darted after her.

Rosy went through the church porch to open the inner door. Some guests were rising from pews and gathering belongings. Several turned curiously to look her way. No one stood at the altar – so Jack hadn't arrived. Her mother grabbed her elbow.

'I'm so sorry. He said he couldn't go through with it,' she said.

Rosy spun around. 'What? Did he say that to you?'

'Yes, he was here very briefly. I had no idea what was going on. Then he left.'

'Did you ask him why?' Rosy couldn't breathe.

'Come on.' Her father laid his palms on both of their backs. He suddenly looked old. 'Joan, you take Rosy back to the hotel. I'll go in and speak to the guests.'

Rosy fled along the walkway back to the hotel. She was hampered by her mother clinging to her arm. Rosy wanted to run, but not just to the room where moments ago she had been excitedly getting ready.

Without halting, she asked, 'Is Jack alright? Where did he say he was going? I just need to speak to him.'

The staff behind the hotel reception looked startled, but she just marched past. In the bedroom, bridesmaid Tanya tried to help. She reached out for Rosy, but that was no comfort.

Rosy plucked at the frothy white layers of her dress. 'I need to get away from all this.' She ripped the veil from her mop of curls. The dress lay on the carpet like a collapsing meringue.

She caught Tanya's arm. 'I can't stay here. I can't face the guests. I need to get home. Will you come with me?'

Her mother, Joan sat on the bed. 'Do you want us to come down to Somerset? I don't like to think of you on your own. We could come just for the next few weeks?'

'No, your flights back to Spain are booked. I know you need to get back. At least I'll feel at home in Somerset and anyway Tanya will be with me.'

Joan wrung her hands, 'I suppose so. And you've got Stella. She's not far away and she would pop around. She's a good sort.'

Rosy nodded. When she was small, the family had lived in Somerset and Stella had been their teenage babysitter. Later the family moved away for Rosy's father's job.

Tanya had changed out of her bridesmaid dress and said, 'But what about you and Jack?'

Rosy shook her head as though trying to dislodge an annoying fly. Somerset was also where Rosy and her fiancé Jack had returned to build up their business. No doubt Jack would turn up there too. Since she had settled there with Jack dear old Stella had become nothing but a busybody, but oh well, it made her mother feel more comfortable to think that Stella would help.

As much to reassure her mother as to answer Tanya, she said, 'I'll be fine. I don't know whether Jack's going to go back home too. I hope he doesn't think he's going to walk in there without answering a lot of questions.' She couldn't turn off her feelings for him, but at the same time her hurt felt like a gnawing stomach-ache. 'I'm sure I'll feel better as soon as I'm away from here.'

Joan hesitated, looking unconvinced, but at that moment Rosy's father arrived and offered to carry the bags to the car.

Once on the road, Rosy stayed silent. She couldn't process anything. They were driving into the setting sun so it was irritating when it shone below the sun visors. The tarmac was still slick from an earlier shower, so Tanya probably thought that she was concentrating on the road. Questions were racing through her mind. How long had Jack been having doubts? Was anyone else involved? Had he ever loved her?

Eventually she exploded with words. 'There must be someone else involved. But who? He'd seemed to be okay, hadn't he, when you saw him? It makes you wonder – did he ever really love me?'

Tanya said, 'He was always chilled. Of course, he must have loved you.'

Rosy barely heard Tanya's soothing tones. 'We were supposed to be flying out to Turkey this evening. We needed that holiday. We'd paid for a balcony with sea view. All the money we spent. I don't suppose we'll get a refund.' Rosy shook her head. 'And the plans for the old bakery – all that time spent renovating it. He's ruined it. I can't see how we can launch the tea shop now.'

'I know hun, all your dreams for a future. I didn't get to see you much in the last few months. Maybe all that work and the wedding got to you both? Perhaps he'll come to his senses now the pressure's off,' Tanya said.

'He'd have to have an exceptionally good excuse for this. No there couldn't be an excuse good enough. I could never trust him again. He didn't even stay to explain.'

They stopped at traffic lights in the centre of a small town. 'What about our money?' Rosy said quietly, her fingers drumming on the steering wheel. 'I'll need to speak to the bank. I'll show him. I can make a go of it on my own,' Rosy said, 'well I have to.' It was said defiantly, yet being without him was like losing one of her arms.

4

As they reached the countryside she loved, Rosy stared out at the now darkening hedges occasionally lit up by her headlights. She and Tanya tried to imagine the conversation at the reception after they had gone. She felt awful that her parents had had to face everyone and deal with the hotel. It had taken them years to get over the death of her brother Alex, and now this. Once her father retired, they'd moved to Spain and built a new life. Rosy was afraid that her situation would cause them anguish all over again.

She tried to focus inwards for a moment. If she couldn't summon all of her positivity, she was scared that she'd sink. She needed to pull it together again so that she could put on a brave face for the people who knew them in the village.

CHAPTER 2

They had had a lot of wine last night, but surely not that much? The duvet was wedged between the mattress and the wrought iron bedstead. Rosy found herself wrapped in the sheet. The empty pillow beside her, brought back the pain. She looked at the stark white ceiling while steeling herself to face a new day of this living nightmare. When she suddenly moved her head, she felt unsteady.

The night before, the bakehouse had been echoey and cold. She had brought out bottles of wine and packets of crisps. Tanya must have recovered well. She could hear her slamming cupboard doors in the kitchen below. Rosy went to the window. Her bedroom was at the back of the bakehouse while the front half of the building was now a newly renovated café. Rosy parted the curtains and saw the Volkswagen Polo below on the gravel drive. The villagers of Sedgeborough expected them to be away for the wedding and honeymoon so if they noticed the car, they might come to check on her. She needed to be ready for visitors.

Too late, there were already voices at the door, Tanya's and another female voice. As she threw on clothes she yelled, 'I'll be down in a minute.'

'No worries. I'm just making coffee,' Tanya called up.

'Yes, don't rush,' came Stella's voice.

Clattering down the open tread staircase, Rosy realised that Stella was standing just below waiting for her.

'I thought I saw your car. Tanya's filled me in about the wedding. I'm so sorry.' Her arms reached out. 'Anything I can do to help - anything at all.'

Rosy's jaw clenched. Somehow Stella always caused this reaction.

'Stella's brought us some milk so we can make a drink,' Tanya called.

The smell of coffee pervaded the cottage. Tanya had brought out the cafetiere. That was cheering. Rosy said, 'Ah thank you Stella. A lifesaver.'

She sank into a deep armchair to let Tanya wait on her. If only she had tried to tame her wild hair before coming down. As usual Stella, wore her blond hair neatly bobbed and her well-ironed jeans and crisp, checked blouse were neat rather than country casual.

Stella looked eager to hear more. Rosy said, 'As you've heard, things didn't go to plan. I'm just getting my head around running this place by myself.'

'I see, and you don't know what caused the rift?'

Rosy grunted in a non-committal way and carried on sipping coffee.

Stella leant towards her, 'I thought maybe, as the café had been a joint project, you'd go back to your old job again. Early days to make any decisions though really. Your head must be reeling.' She brushed Rosy's hand.

Rosy suppressed a shiver. 'I've invested a lot of my life into this and . . .yes, I think I should make a go of it.'

'Good on you.' Stella nodded, her eyes gleaming with interest.

'Thank you, I'm so lucky to have friends here.' She cast a look at Tanya.

'We all stick together in Sedgeborough. Come along to the Businesswomen's Lunch. The third Thursday of every month. They'll all be there for you. Local bed and breakfast owners sent their guests down to the farm as a result of meeting me at the group.' She turned to Tanya, 'You should come to the farm too. I rent an outbuilding at Manor Farm for a Museum of Wetlands Life. It's only £4 per head for visitors.'

That galvanised Tanya to leap up. 'I know, Rosy, let's look around the 'Spotted Teapot' now. You know, I haven't seen the renovations. We can work out what else needs to be done, and then maybe we can help?'

Rosy was in a fog. Tanya's enthusiasm jarred her out of it. The business had been their baby. It might feel like visiting the tattered remains of their relationship. Tanya lifted the key from a hook just beside the door to the front shop. When it was unlocked, they were met by a musty smell. Not what Rosy had expected. She wondered whether she could face seeing the catering kitchen again.

Stella swivelled around in the centre of the kitchen. 'It's unrecognisable.' She sounded wistful. 'You didn't keep the old baker's oven then?'

'I know it meant such a lot when your family owned the bakehouse Stella, but it wasn't right for our needs.' Rosy saw the kitchen through Stella's eyes with its stainless-steel surfaces gleaming under recessed lights. She couldn't help a little smile as she led them out to the seating area. The light oak wooden flooring and white painted furniture made the most of light from tiny-paned bay windows. Rosy ran her fingers along the smoothness of the oak serving counter, then tipped the empty wicker baskets on a display stand to look inside. She moved behind the counter to reposition the chalk boards. It was charming. All it needed was cakes, and perhaps flowers on the tables.

'Wow this is awesome. It's so lovely,' Tanya gushed. 'It could be open in no time. What do you think of it, Stella?'

'Yes,' Stella nodded slowly, 'it is very nice. I'm just looking at that picture over on the far wall.' It was a painting in oils showing Sedgeborough's high street complete with a horse-drawn cart, women in long dresses and branches reaching over the stone wall of Manor Farm.

'I know. We found it in the loft here. It seems ideal for the wall of a tea shop. We changed the frame for something more rustic,' Rosy said. 'Of course, you maybe remember it from when your family lived here?'

'Yes, I think I do,' Stella said abruptly, striding towards the front door. Her urge to leave was thwarted, as it was locked.

'Don't worry I'll open it for you.' Rosy released her then stood on the doorstep to wave her off.

Tanya pulled a face. 'I'm not sure about her.'

'The Bakehouse has been in her family for years. She was very friendly when we bought it from her, but hmm I'm not sure why but, it's like she's jealous. She's got a hidden agenda or something.'

'We're seeing plots everywhere.' Tanya dug Rosy in the ribs. 'Anyway, I'm going to leave you to sort out business here, while I do a food shop for you. Something you can quickly prepare when you're on your own.'

'Yes, and I need to contact the bank,' Rosy said, 'But it sounds like you're planning to leave me.'

She felt hollow feeling at the thought of being alone, but she wouldn't admit it to Tanya. A few days later, she drove Tanya to the railway station. 'Come back and visit really soon, won't you,' she said.

'Of course, I will come for a holiday and I bet that by then the 'Spotted Teapot' will be a thriving business. You will be all right on your own, won't you?'

'Of course I will.' Rosy laughed.

The following day, Rosy checked the bedside drawers, scoured the kitchen cupboards and even hunted for Jack's belongings underneath furniture. She steeled herself against finding a clue as to what had gone wrong between them, but there was nothing incriminating. Everything got thrown into black plastic bags and piled up in the living room.

So many memories. She felt the wiry texture of his

overcoat against her cheek. She had snuggled up to that overcoat so often – in a horse drawn carriage on holiday in Austria and then, watching lights reflected in the Thames after a day's Christmas shopping. It was difficult to square the Jack that she loved with the man who had betrayed her.

She lingered over photographs, particularly pictures of herself and Jack on nights out with her brother Alex. She couldn't give up those, so she held them back. She cradled Jack's tool bag. The tools would be useful. She was tempted to hold onto them too, but they were his, so she added the bag to the pile.

When she sat at the table for lunch the sight of all his belongings made her stomach churn. She escaped to a wicker chair in the glass lean-to at the rear of the cottage. The sun's heat warmed her despite being filtered through the leaves of the apple trees. In the beginning she had rejoiced in the wilderness of rough grass and fruit trees, but now all that mowing would be her job. The phone pinged in her apron pocket. It was a WhatsApp from Jack.

'We need to talk. I hope you're OK. I'm on my way to the village. Don't worry, I've booked in at Manor Farm.'

This was unbearable. Rosy sat hunched over the phone. So, he'd be with Hyacinth and her family at the Manor Farm B & B. As Stella was working in the Wetlands Museum attached to the farm, she would relish a front seat to their relationship break up too.

CHAPTER 3

A text message pinged. It was Jack to announce that he was on his way. So now he wouldn't even pick up the phone to speak? Rosy's shoulders tightened. She manipulated her jaw in an effort to relax it.

She needed to ask the important questions. When did he start to have doubts? Why had he left it so late to tell her? Leaving it until the wedding date seemed a deliberate humiliation. What was he planning to do in the future? He'd spent so long renovating the café and planning the business with her. Surely he would be expecting her to be furious. He had wrecked everything, so he had better be suffering too. She paced from the kitchen to the tea shop door and back again. As he had had time to consider his options, his life was probably still on track.

With a series of rumbles across the gravel, a Land Rover drew up beside the cottage. He must have borrowed the vehicle from the farm. She guessed he would be nervous about seeing her. If she screamed at him, she guessed he would disappear as quickly as possible. She needed to keep outwardly cool and be logical.

Jack tried the door and then she heard him putting his key into the lock and opening it. She could feel indignation rising in her chest.

'You don't have the right to walk straight in on me,' she burst out. 'Hand over your key.'

Jack's eyebrows shot up. 'I still own half of this building, but okay,' he raised his hands as if in surrender, 'I'll knock in future.'

He appeared relaxed but then, he usually hid his true feelings and relied on turning on the charm. When his gaze fell upon the pile of black bags he scratched the back of his neck. 'Ah thanks love. You've got my stuff ready. Let's make this as easy as possible for the both of us.'

'What?' she was annoyed with herself: her voice had risen. 'How can it be easy. Nothing about this is easy. You've still given no explanation. Are you planning to stay at Manor Farm for long?'

He took a couple of steps back. 'I can't tell you. I haven't got anywhere else yet.'

'Perhaps you should have thought of that...'

'I know. I'm sorry,' he said quickly. She was thrown by this. He looked like a dog that knows that it shouldn't take food from the table. At one time she might have found his expression appealing but now it was fuel to the flames of her anger. Just in time, she remembered her plan to stay cool and ask logical questions.

Pulling out a dining chair, she drew in a deep breath and sat down. 'There has to be someone else, Jack. So, who is she and when did it all start?'

'Huh?' Without looking at her, he made a move towards his possessions.

'Come on, you owe me that.' She simply had to raise her

voice, to stop him breezing through this. 'Tell me what happened. There was no hint that you were going to back out of the wedding.'

His eyes shifted from the skirting board to the window. 'If I knew more, I'd tell you more. I'm suffering too, you know. All I can say is it just didn't feel right.'

'Feel right. . .'

'You know. You have to question everything at times like that. Look I'll get these bags in the car and come back for the rest.' He picked up one in each hand and disappeared out of the door. She heard gravel crunch and the slam of a vehicle door. He was going to come back, wasn't he? As she rushed to the door, he returned.

He would be leaving any moment and she'd be left with her thoughts. 'I loved you enough to want to spend our lives together. Did you ever love me?'

He turned for a briefcase full of his papers, his tennis racket and the tool bag. She snatched at his arm. 'Well did you. Did you love me, Jack?' She picked up the briefcase and flung it across the floor. Then went for the tool bag. Jack grasped her arm to stop her.

She screeched, 'If you ever loved me, as you said you did, how could you do this to me?'

There was a look of sympathy, or pity, on his face. That look ripped into her. He smoothed his hair down behind his ear. 'I suppose I must have loved you at one time. Perhaps it was all this,' he waved at the building, 'that drove us apart.' Jack shook his head. 'Maybe we were always better at friendship than romance. And you left me to do everything so . . . well, people in the village,' then he faltered. 'I did all the negotiating with Stella's family to buy this place. That took some doing. Sometimes I talked it through with other people – with your parents - as much as with you.'

He had seemed to want to take the lead. He had been a perfect fit with her family. Tears came to her eyes. 'You knew Alex when he was alive. He'd accepted you as part of our family. Perhaps that's it. You're running away from our family now that it's fractured without him.'

He stopped, breathing heavily, and muttered something under his breath. Then he said, 'C'mon I know you're hurt – course you are. I'm going to make the split as easy as I can.'

It was bubbling up inside. This wasn't easy, it was gut wrenchingly difficult. Pictures of the wedding venue, her parents and guests flew through her mind. She let out a screaming cry, wailing with her mouth wide. 'Did I deserve this?' she was full of tears and turned for the kitchen roll. 'Jack?'

As she blew her nose, he said, 'There was so much playing on my mind but I'm sorry I left it so late.' He sighed. 'Look let me get this lot shifted and then we'll have a proper talk.'

He came back and drew a chair up beside her. 'We made a great team. I hope we don't lose touch with each other.'

Rosy could barely take in what he was saying, she was in

full flow of tears. She turned her head away. She didn't believe that he really cared. He just wanted to make a smooth getaway.

He said, 'We need to sort out some details. I want an up-to-date valuation of this building and then we can work out how to split it. I could take this place on if you want me to, but if you're hoping to stay here then you'll need to buy me out.'

He rattled on as he dismantled their dreams. She grabbed the kitchen roll and tried to control her sobs.

'I can't face thinking about the money. What about the wedding costs?' She briefly covered her face in her hands.

When she looked again, he was flushed and had shifted a little further away. His swept back hair and brown eyes looked just as appealing as ever. She had touched a nerve.

He said, 'I know. We'll take those costs into account when we make a settlement. I take it you want to run this place?'

'You bet I bloody do.' She jutted out her chin and screwed the tissue up in her hand.

'You do. I'll get my solicitor onto it.'

She wasn't sure why the word solicitor was such a trigger. She lay her forehead on the table. He said, 'Take care of yourself.'

She heard the door and realised he had walked out. Rosy rushed for the door. He was climbing into the Land Rover. He started the engine. He gave a brief wave before he reversed away.

She crammed her fist into her mouth.

CHAPTER 4

Rosy woke up with sore eyes and with pressure that felt like fingers clamping her head. She slept badly. The conversation played over in her mind while she fixed up breakfast. She spit out words like 'patronising', 'the audacity of the man', 'he can think again'. He still hadn't convinced her that there wasn't some woman in the background.

Determined to show him the cost of the wedding, she pored over her diary for records of deposits, cash purchases and contracts. Each one brought a lump to her throat. She even forgot to have lunch. She would only be satisfied once she had handed the itemised costs to Jack. Grabbing an apple, Rosy left the house. She enjoyed biting into its crispness. A robin landed on a wall to look at her. It fluttered ahead along the High Street and perched in a tree before flying away again.

Manor Farm and its outbuildings were not far. It made sense for Jack to stay there as Hyacinth ran a farmhouse bed and breakfast. The family had just started a small garden centre too, while Hyacinth's son and his wife worked with the dairy herd.

In the gateway Rosy glanced in the direction of the Wetlands Museum, but there was no sign of Stella; she was probably busy. Hyacinth, and her husband Brian, were usually around in the daytime. Rosy could hear the barking of farm dogs. Hyacinth was probably over sixty, but she still did hard physical work. Rosy found her using a sack trolley to move bags of compost across the paved courtyard. She was wearing jeans with a belt slung low around her hips and a clingy T-shirt. She stopped and brushed her long, still dark, hair out of her eyes as she called the dogs and strode towards Rosy. Even with soil-caked boots her high cheekbones and long stride gave her a model elegance.

'Hello. How are you?' Rosy called.

'Not too bad.' Hyacinth took off her gardening gloves and laid them on the wall. She looked over her shoulder. 'Um Rosy, you know we've got Jack staying here? I'm so sorry about your wedding.'

'Yes I knew he was staying. Thank you. Actually, I came to see him. Is he around?'

'Mm I don't think he's here at the moment, but come in and have a cup of tea.'

Rosy had been to the farmhouse with Jack many times before. The lines of muddy wellingtons and dog beds just inside the door were familiar. There was a cluttered working kitchen. It was the family space; paying guests used the front door.

Rosy watched Hyacinth putting on the kettle. She began to feel awkward at the thought that Jack could walk in at any moment and Hyacinth was being put in the middle of the two of them.

When Hyacinth turned to her, she said, 'So have you thought what you're going to do now?'

Rosy sighted, 'I don't know. Carry on, I suppose.'

'Difficult for you both, hey? There are no winners.' Hyacinth started to say something else and then stopped short.

Rosy, already feeling fragile, sensed that Hyacinth felt caught between the two of them. At that moment, the phone rang.

Hyacinth shook her head in annoyance. 'It'll be the business. The phone's going all day.'

'Oh, well don't worry,' Rosy gabbled, 'I'll write Jack's name on the note and leave it here for him. You take the phone call.' She folded the invoice and put it on the kitchen table as Hyacinth answered the phone.

❋ ❋ ❋

A good walk would clear her head. Even though she knew she ought to get the tea shop valued, it seemed an enormous step. She turned off the High Street and down one of the twisting lanes that looped away from it. Rows of cottage windows were in darkness, reflecting the now dull sky. Peeping over the wall of a garden she admired the orderly display of dahlias dancing in the breeze, but then noticed that the same breeze had swept in a cigarette packet and pieces of paper.

Further along the street was a cottage garden bursting with astilbes, roses, and tall phlox. The cottage was often rented out to holidaymakers, but it had been empty for a while. Now she noticed a man standing in the doorway. She thought he might be in his early fifties, wavy hair, greying at the temples, high cheekbones in a long face. His abstracted look, his stubble, and his waistcoat buttoned up wrongly made her think that he wasn't a holiday renter. She wondered about asking if he was all right, but even if he wasn't, she didn't feel up to offering support to anyone.

He raised his hand in greeting as she reached the garden wall.

She called, 'Hello, I'm glad the cottage isn't empty anymore. Have you been here long?' She paused at the gate.

He looked distinguished and disreputable at the same time. Slowly rubbing his forehead with one hand, he gripped the doorframe, slightly swaying. Was he drunk? In a cultured voice he said, 'Pleased to meet you. Yes, I've been here for a few days.'

'Welcome to Sedgeborough. I'm Rosy.'

'Pleased to meet you, Rosy. I'm just settling in, or I would be able to welcome you in for a visit.'

'No worries. I run a café called the "Spotted Teapot" We're not quite open yet but I'm always working in there if you want to drop in.'

'That's useful to know. So, you are relatively new here yourself?'

'Well, it's a long story, but I lived in the village when I was at school, then we moved away. Just over a year ago I came back to buy the old bakery. We'd been renovating it, but I'm on my own now.' She couldn't avoid letting her smile falter. She hoped he hadn't noticed.

'I'm sorry to hear that. I suppose we are in the peak tourist season, so you probably feel under some pressure to open the business.'

'That's true. I need a boost now before it goes quiet in Autumn. I'm going to try to attract locals into the café as well though. Any ideas would be welcome.'

He had stepped off the front doorstep wearing his leather slippers. 'I'll give it some thought as I drive around the area.'

Rosy warmed to him. 'That's kind of you. You're going to be here for a while then?'

'Yes, I'm,' he stopped and looked back towards the door. 'Oh, if you can close your eyes to disarray, would you care to come in for a while and we can share some marketing ideas now.'

He seemed pleasant enough and Rosy really needed human contact.

He had to dip his head to step through the door of the cottage.

'I should have introduced myself, I'm Ken.' He held out a hand. It felt dry and cool.

The traditional cottage matched his old-world charm.

'What do you think of Sedgeborough, Ken,' Rosy gestured to the ceiling light drilled into a beam, 'It's dim in these cottages with their thick walls and tiny windows, but I'm a fan of old cottages.'

He raised his dark eyebrows and nodded. 'I'm sure I will be able to create a welcoming atmosphere, but it needs tender loving care. Do sit down while I assemble a tray for coffee.'

Rosy noticed the unlit cast-iron stove, a scarf hanging over the end of the stair rail, and, on a table beside an armchair, a pipe with a packet of pipe tobacco. She took a seat on a chintz sofa.

'I hope you like the coffee. I order a speciality coffee monthly.' He was more at ease as a host than he had been when standing in the garden. Then he continued as though he'd been in the middle of an explanation, 'Yes, I needed a break and so I applied for a sabbatical to study the barrows of Somerset. The burial mounds rather than the garden variety.' He laughed at his own joke, 'I'm going to stay here for almost a year.'

'You'll be practically a resident then. So where were you working before?'

'Ah, I'm part of the university archaeology department. I'm interested in what the local people know of the barrows, the oral folk legends and how they relate to people's lives now.'

She racked her brains for any insight. 'I know tourists like to climb the Burrow Mump to photograph the view. That's near here of course and I've heard people talk about Priddy Nine Barrows. Hyacinth at the farm, her family have lived here for generations. It might be worth talking to her.'

He rubbed his hands together, 'Of course, it will be an excellent way to get to know my neighbours. If I may, I could arrange to meet with people at your café and that would bring you extra custom. Have you got a written marketing plan?'

Rosy flushed, she needed to be more professional. 'No, but I'm planning to have a Grand Opening. Something different so that I can invite the press.'

'If you'd care to let me help, just let me know,' he said.

CHAPTER 5

Ken became a regular visitor to the 'Spotted Teapot', even before it officially opened. Rosy found it refreshing to chat with someone who had never known Jack. Ken provided a sounding board for her business plans and as he got to know her better, he grew less stuffy. She wished she knew more about the ancient history of Somerset so that she could return the favour.

One morning he arrived freshly shaven, smartly dressed and carrying a leather briefcase. As she let him through the front door she thought, 'he's taking this seriously.' Their footsteps sounded hollow. The tea shop was empty. She could focus everything on their conversation. They huddled around a laptop at one of the tables to create an improved marketing plan. Working with him felt like sitting in a deep easy chair sipping a mug of hot chocolate with cream.

Rosy had chosen to hold the launch on a Saturday in a few weeks' time - a tight deadline. She had already ordered advertising fliers from a printer.

'Tourists are just passing trade, so I've aimed my fliers at the villagers,' she said. 'I need to catch the parents who drop their children off at school in the mornings. Perhaps I should offer a discount for customers who arrive before 10am.'

'Good idea. You could advertise groups too. Something

like a book group,' he said.

Rosy smiled into his eyes. 'Thank you for spending so much time on this. It's very good of you.'

'I'm enjoying it. It's such a refreshing change from. . .' They were both startled by a sudden knocking on the window.

'Hello,' Stella peered through the glass and then gestured to the front door. Rosy got up to let her in. 'I was just passing, and I saw people here. Are you open then?'

'Not really.' Rosy softened it with a smile. 'We're just doing some paperwork, but come in.' She opened the door wider.

Seeing Stella was a reminder of the farm. Rosy just managed to stop herself asking about Jack. He still took up too much of her thoughts. She went to organise refreshments in the kitchen. She could hear Ken and Stella getting to know each other. As Rosy returned with the coffee cups chinking in their saucers, Stella picked up the design for the flier and said, 'I notice your Launch Date is the same day as our Farm and Museum Open Day.'

'Oh?' Rosy hadn't heard anything about an Open day and couldn't remember seeing any advertising.

'Yes, we've got a face painter for the children, hog roast, craft stalls and displays.'

'Hmm.' Ken looked thoughtful.

Stella wrinkled her nose. 'Oh dear. But don't worry. I'm sure people will come on to see the "Spotted Teapot" after they've left us.'

What would Ken think at her lack of research into possible clashes? Rosy felt her ears going red. Would people really attend both? If they'd been to a hog roast, would they care about the launch of a café? Ken was busy asking polite questions about the museum and he promised Stella that he would visit. Then she had to leave to reopen it.

Once Stella had left, Ken said, 'You look downhearted.'

Rosy gave a rueful laugh. 'That's because I am. I've got all the fliers printed so I can't change the date. I wonder if anyone's going to come.'

He touched her hand lightly. 'I'm sure people will be curious to see what you've done here. We'll have to make this an impactful Launch Day.'

Her hand tingled at his touch. She liked hearing the 'we'll'. She had been feeling so alone.

* * *

Rosy struggled to get up each morning, she knew she had to work frantically. She began to put in late nights to try to meet her own deadline.

A local balloon company would be good for outdoor decorations. Then she discovered her old bicycle, complete with basket, in the garage. It needed an overhaul. She brought it out and gave it a brush up. It looked vintage. She could display it, garlanded with flowers, on the cobbles in front of the tea shop. She looked up florists. Most of them were busy with weddings that day, but eventually Daniel Harris, Florists and Greengrocers, remembered that he'd known Rosy at school and agreed to meet the deadline.

'Gotta get live music,' she muttered under her breath. There was Nicola, a friend of the family who played folk guitar. Nicola sounded surprised but enthusiastic on the phone. Rosy felt like jumping up and down. In fact when she rang off, she gave a whoop. If only Jack could see her now.

Local cookery writer Annette Thomas agreed to bring some of her books along and to cut the opening ribbon. That prompted Ken to suggest that the tea shop could host a book exchange for patrons to browse and borrow second-hand books.

He arrived on launch day carrying a grocery carton loaded with books with his toolbox lodged on top. Ken stayed for the morning to put up the new bookshelves.

There was hardly a moment to draw in the toasty vanilla scent of freshly baked cakes. The celebrity writer was due at any moment, but Rosy couldn't resist trying one. Call it quality control. It was golden with a fine texture. Moist and sweet on her tongue.

She had just brushed the crumbs from her clothes when she noticed Nicola at the door with her guitar.

'Rosy how are you?' Nicola held Rosy's forearm. 'And how are your mum and dad? First losing Alex and then I was devastated to hear about your wedding. I'm so sorry. How must you be feeling?' Rosy didn't want to dwell on that now. She had to stay positive, and she was aware of Ken turning away politely. She gabbled news of her parents and, to brush over the awkward moment, she offered Nicola a cake. Ken set up a stool for Nicola and tidied away her guitar case. Soon the soft strumming of music created a relaxed atmosphere.

Annette Thomas was parking her black Mini just outside. Rosy left via the side door and jogged around to the cobbled forecourt to meet her. She took a look down the High Street, there was a steady trail of people walking down to Manor Farm. She blinked hard and concentrated on welcoming Annette.

Over the lunch period they had four more customers. Rosy's mind wandered to the Farm Open Day. She wondered if Jack had been there.

'Well, it looks like the Farm Open Day might have nabbed all our customers. I could cry,' Rosy said under her breath to Ken.

'Was there a Farm Open Day today?' he asked.

An attempt at dry humour? He didn't look as though he were joking. 'Ha, ha,' Rosy said.

'Oh, I apologise. I'd hate to offend you.'

'Don't worry. I'm just feeling a bit down.'

'Don't give up yet.' He grabbed a plate of cakes and swished out of the front door. What was he up to?

From the window, she watched him leave just as a dilapidated bus decorated by swirls of purple paint, screeched to a halt behind Annette's mini. So, the bicycle with geraniums cascading from the front basket and the balloons around the tearoom doorway proved to be an effective traffic stopper after all. The passenger door of the old bus swung open. A spaniel-haired girl clung onto the door handle and swung out.

They could just hear her say, 'Hey a cute tea shop.'

The driver joined her, his dreadlocks swinging. He loped across the cobbled frontage.

Rosy bristled with wary interest. The doorbell dinged to announce her as she went out to see them. She stood framed by decorative balloons and flowers.

'Hello. Can I help you?'

The lanky man looked up from his examination of the bike and smiled. 'Yeh, cool. I'm Luke. I think we could help each other.' He beckoned his passenger to join them.

'C'mon Mandy.' Then Luke gestured to the old bike, 'I could repair this old thing... and anything else that needs upcycling. It's one of my specialities.'

Rosy reasoned that she should be open to possibilities. She hoped her neighbours were as open-minded as she was.

'Well step inside. It's our Launch Day. Come and have a coffee.'

They seemed to fill the room with energy until she persuaded them to sit. They were immediately drawn to the folk guitar.

'D'you know any Bob Marley.' Luke pleaded and Nicola obliged and even added her own version of 'You can get it if you really want' as an encore. Rosy felt for Annette, who had gone a bit quiet. Of course, no one was buying cookery books.

The bell dinged again, as Ken reappeared followed by a couple of families with their children and four or five young teenagers. She jumped to serve them all and the atmosphere warmed up.

'I'll get the Cokes for the kids,' Ken said.

'Thanks Ken.' Rosy gave him the biggest smile.

'Mm don't thank me yet. I think I may have made us some enemies. The farm family were pleasant enough, but Stella and her younger brother. She didn't impress me. Her face was so sour, that I think it encouraged some of these families to leave with me.'

She didn't think that Stella had a brother. Who could that be? Rosy had no more time to think, as at that moment Nicola struck up 'We shall overcome' loudly which made Mandy and Luke from the bus cheer. Annette made her way through the customers, to tap Rosy on the arm, 'It's getting a little rowdy for me now. Thank you for asking me.' Rosy accompanied her to the door to see her out.

When it grew quieter, Rosy had a chat with each new family and tried to engage with the teenagers. Then she gestured towards Ken and introduced the newcomers from the bus. He was unfazed; in fact, he seemed to relax.

Of course, he was accustomed to scruffy young archaeology students at the university. Luke sat down, his long legs stretched out in front of him, while Mandy wandered around the room.

Ken began to explain his research subject to Luke. Luke's face lit up. 'Yeh man, I'm interested in dowsing the ley lines. Everything centres around Glastonbury.'

'It does. Of course, we would have been on a series of promontories and islands at the time that these ancient sites were created. I'd like to hear your views on them. If you're still around and want to come out with me sometime, you would be welcome,' Ken said. Such an unlikely friendship.

Mandy stopped in front of the oil painting that Stella had noticed earlier. 'Awesome. Is this a picture of old Sedgeborough? Can't you just imagine our bus as a horse drawn caravan and a little delivery boy using that old bike?'

Rosy smiled at her. 'I know! I often picture the High Street of old.'

'So, the old bike,' Luke said, 'I meant what I said. I could renovate it. I'm good with machinery and I can sand down furniture and paint it white like your tables here.'

'Are you looking for work?' Ken asked.

'Suppose I might be,' Luke muttered.

'And I'm an artist,' Mandy gave an unexpected twirl so that her skirt swirled. 'I can embroider old clothes and tie-die material to create funky accessories. Murals are my thing too.'

'I'm afraid there's no spare money to pay staff,' Rosy said. In fact, she could see that Nicola had begun to help out by passing around cakes.

'But maybe you could attract people to the "Spotted Teapot" to undertake a recycling project, learn art skills, buy recycled products – and use the café at the same time,' Ken said. He looked at their visitors. 'Perhaps a joint enterprise?'

'Sounds good to me,' Luke said, 'As long as you realise that it might be short term for us. We like to split when we get itchy feet.'

Rosy's heart leapt. 'Fantastic. Thank you everyone. I can see the "Spotted Teapot" as the hub of the community.'

CHAPTER 6

The sheets and tablecloths hanging on the line between apple trees felt gloriously warm to touch. Rosy caressed her cheek with one of them then, stopped to investigate a tiny morse code chirrup, but the grass was so long and thick that she couldn't spot any crickets.

She was carrying the laundry basket on the way back to the cottage when Ken came down the gravelled drive. Her spirits lifted. He followed her inside and took off his rucksack. Rosy raised an eyebrow.

He laughed. 'I've brought cider. I've come to catch up with my new friend Luke, but,' he stopped theatrically, 'I've been delving into the traditional recipes of Somerset and I wondered if you'd allow me to bake a cake for you?'

Was there no end to the unexpected sides of his personality? 'Of course, you can have a go,' she said, 'I didn't know that you had an interest.'

'Baking relaxes me, and maybe if you like my Somerset Cider and Apple Cake, I can bake for the tea shop. I'd enjoy bringing my talents to the venture.'

She grinned, wondering whether he was angling for a change of career. She'd reserve judgement. He unloaded the bottles onto her table.

'And Luke is out in the garage,' she said. 'But tell me, how was your trip?'

ROSY'S RECYCLING TEA SHOP

'Trip?'

'You were looking around Glastonbury?'

Ken paused and examined the label on a bottle. Rosy noted he had stubble again. Perhaps he was growing a beard. There were a few stray, grey hairs around his ears and temples. His eyebrows in contrast were thick and dark brown. Rosy remembered Jack's brows. She'd always thought he was so vain, plucking any stray hairs that didn't fit the smooth brow line.

Ken looked up and sighed. 'Oh yes, was I? Well, I drove to Langport and wandered around the shops. No long barrows there, so I won't be returning anytime soon.'

He grimaced and glanced towards the window. 'I must block out an afternoon in my diary to spend some time in Glastonbury. My memory isn't what it was.'

She looked to see what had caught his attention outside, but there was nothing there except a glint of sunlight through the leaves.

'In confidence Rosy, I'm concerned. My poor memory is affecting my work. I've found ways around it. I write everything down, but I am seriously wondering how I can continue in my post at the university.'

Rosy picked stray pegs out of her washing to allow time to think. Maybe he really was turning to baking as an option. His voice was flat. It sounded worrying.

'That must be upsetting.'

'Mm hum I feel out of control. I wonder how long it's

going to be before I completely lose it. I can see myself as a dribbling halfwit.' He gave a little laugh.

She didn't join him. 'Now come on, don't talk like that.'

He scratched behind his ear, fidgeting. 'I have a good portion of my life still ahead and since moving here, I've a new purpose, but worry over this – this condition has put all that on hold.'

She wanted to hear more but Ken was a private person and if he had wanted to tell her what his new purpose was, he would have said more. 'Have you been to a doctor?'

'I wish I hadn't said anything now. I haven't been able to face looking into the problem.'

Poor Ken. She considered keeping quiet but. . . she put her hand on his arm. 'I really think you ought to consult a doctor. To have memory loss so young? It's possible, I know, but it's worth finding out what's causing it.' She tried to communicate sympathy when he met her eyes. 'If there's something wrong, they could do something.'

He cleared his throat and turned abruptly. 'Well, I'll take a break to see how Luke is getting on.' He left the kitchen.

Rosy took a deep breath. She hoped that he wasn't regretting confiding in her. Had she said too much? He seemed isolated by his problems. It echoed her own situation. She missed her parents in Spain, and after Jack wrecked her life, she had felt alone, but things improved rapidly. She was amazed that so many people had been willing to become a part of her life. Yet sometimes she still felt a pang at the loss of Jack and sometimes she distrusted the speed that new friends gathered around. She had always found it difficult to let people in, and now she risked being hurt again.

Mandy invited Rosy to join them at an animal rights meeting that evening. It wasn't far from Sedgeborough and they offered to take her along in their old bus. Rosy shrugged but agreed. She welcomed the distraction, but it had political connotations. She questioned her stance on animal rights. She was certainly open to finding out more.

It was interesting to see how they'd adapted the bus. The seats were covered in crushed velvet and cooking pans were secured by bungy cords. She wondered what it was like in winter. It would probably be icy.

The group met on the upper floor of a pub. Dipping her head to look through the dormer windows, Rosy could see the roofs of genteel stone houses on the opposite side of the street. The group dragged a mishmash of old armchairs and stools into the middle of the room as more folk stomped up the staircase to join them.

Rosy worried that she'd stick out as a newbie. She remembered feeling that way when she'd first joined the Brownies. She didn't look anything like a stereotypical extremist, so she was relieved to see that there was a mixture of people at the meeting. A man with a moustache stepped forward and said, 'Yeh, sit down guys, let's get started.'

He had a word for each person and a quick greeting for

Rosy. They were seemed nice. The discussion focused on where to get the best vegan burgers. One of the younger girls had a news update on her dog's new litter of puppies. As the conversation grew more serious Rosy could see that they were passionate about stopping cruelty. A young girl thumped her fist on the table when she explained that she had been reading about experiments on animals. Rosy would ask Ken whether he knew what they did at the university.

She was being won over but still questioning. She asked, 'You haven't seen this yourself though?'

An older man with a long white beard stiffened and his jaw hardened. The girl, looked away from her. 'How do you think we'd get to see it? Unless we went to work there.'

'I was just wondering.' Rosy saw Mandy look down as she and Luke shifted in their seats. She decided to keep quiet and listen. She would have liked to know if they had evidence that the tests were unwarranted but decided not to cause controversy.

In the car park, they said their farewells. Rosy enthusiastically agreed that she would join them for the next meeting. She had been so uplifted by being part of a group that she didn't doubt their friendliness, but on the way home she wondered if there had been a cooling among the group when she asked questions. In the old days she would have been going home to Jack and she would have been able to confide in him. Losing him had shaken her confidence in meeting people.

CHAPTER 7

Ken had been invited to the Animal Rights Group, but he wasn't at all interested. She told him about it later. Rosy's friends were split into factions, but at the moment it seemed to be working out. She could see him through the kitchen door, wearing a striped apron, whipping up the lightest of scones and his own Sedgeborough Easter Biscuits. It meant that Rosy was free to meet customers and develop group activities.

She hadn't paid for advertising, but word had gone out that she was going to run craft groups. At the first session there were more participants than she had expected. Even Stella arrived, slightly late and out of breath. Rosy was flattered that she'd taken time off from the museum to join them. Like the Pied Piper, Rosy led them into the back garden where they donned safety glasses and stood well back to watch her smash crockery, ready to make mosaics. Mandy's mosaic designs were on display to inspire the group. Back indoors they gathered at the tables looking expectant. On cue, Ken emerged to take their orders for refreshment. Then there was a hum of activity, lick lipping, and frowns of concentration as each person worked in their own way. Rosy mused that even when everything appeared to be smashed something beautiful could emerge.

Her customers' enthusiasm inspired her to schedule more classes. She would need to sell tickets for the next one to make sure that there was space for everyone. During the lunch break she discussed it with Mandy. Rosy called the local paper on her mobile. She dictated an advert for two new classes: one in tie-dying and another called 'Make your own Sun catcher.' It meant that she missed out on joining the group for their vegetarian, salad lunch. Her stomach rumbled for the rest of the afternoon, but it was worth it. At the end of the day, she discussed her follow-on courses with the group.

When they'd gone, Mandy walked over to see Luke in the garage. He was dragging some fascinating steampunk products outside. Rosy exclaimed at his artistry. There was a sculpture made entirely of keys and a variety of up-cycled planters. He'd used the beauty of the rust in some cases and polished the metal to a high sheen in others. She was surprised at how heavy they were. In the evening, they heaved them into the tea shop to create a display. Most of the smaller items would fly of the shelves.

Stella telephoned the next day.

Rosy was keen to get some feedback from her. 'You were at the mosaic class. Did you enjoy it? I'm sorry I didn't get a chance to have a proper chat with you.'

'Ah yes, it was busy, wasn't it? I enjoyed making mosaics. I think I'll carry on and do some more at home. Thank you,' Stella said. 'We'll get a chance to talk properly later this week anyway. I promised to tell you about our next Business Networking event. It's on Thursday evening, so it won't interfere with your opening hours – although you seem to have gathered quite the collection of people to help you with it now anyway. Well done.'

'Thank you, that's very kind of you.'

Stella continued, 'Wonderful, I'll pick you up at seven if you'd like to come along with me.'

On Thursday evening, Rosy stood in front of her wardrobe biting her lip. She plumped for office-type clothes, a navy skirt with a navy and white patterned blouse. She hoped she didn't look too much like a flight attendant. By the time that Stella arrived, Rosy had found black court shoes to complete the outfit.

On the journey, Stella wanted to gossip about her fellow attendees at the mosaic class and she was full of praise for the vegetarian buffet. They arrived outside a hotel not far from Sedgeborough. Even before they entered the conference room, they could hear the buzz from a crowd of women talking. Rosy was handed a glass of wine and immediately took a large slurp.

People were standing clustered in groups, heels sinking into a thick, beige carpet. Stella melted away immediately, leaving Rosy to survey the huddles of animated women. The high-energy room made her want to slink away, but she took a deep breath, and when she sighted a tiny opening in one of the groups, she edged herself in amongst the bodies. There was a fug of expensive perfume. A few of the women glanced towards her and some mouthed, 'hello' and gave small waves, flashing nails of burgundy, baby pink and light mauve.

At a natural pause, Rosy's nearest neighbours introduced themselves as Grace and Roshana. Grace was a hairdresser and Roshana was an estate agent. They produced their business cards. Rosy made a mental note to get back to her printer to order some for herself. She was so busy wondering whether she had anything in common with them, that she lost the thread of the conversation completely. She should pay attention.

'So, what do you do, Rosy?' Grace was asking.

She told them about 'The Spotted Teapot' and that she was going to run classes there. She was pleased to see their faces light up. 'Perhaps we could have the next one of these at 'The Spotted Teapot,' someone said.

Stella joined their group. 'Ah you're discussing our new little café. It's charming, but I have noticed a, well, a new element among the clientele,' she said with a smirk.

Rosy felt herself growing hot. 'If you mean Mandy and Luke,' she said, including the other women in her glance, 'they're helping me diversify. They're upcycling and creating art pieces. It brings some life to the place. I've been glad of them.' The women were still looking from her to Stella and back, so she injected even more enthusiasm into her voice. 'In fact, you should come and see the wonderful metal sculptures on display.'

'Oh of course, well if you're happy to have "artists" there, but be aware that it could just lower the tone with ladies who lunch and the tourists.' Stella's laugh trilled out.

Rosy gulped. Stella was supposed to be a friend. She smiled. 'Time will tell. So are there any other businesses from Sedgeborough here tonight?' she asked.

Conversation moved on. Rosy made a point of smiling at

everyone as she took a deep breath and said, 'Well I think I'll refill my coffee cup.'

She yearned to go home, but at that moment someone clapped, 'Ladies your attention please. Time for group introductions. Just give your name and a sentence or two to explain your business. If you have leaflets, they can be left on the table by the door.'

Shit, she didn't have leaflets either, but while each person was calling out their name, she mentally prepared something succinct and positive about 'the Spotted Teapot'. When her turn came she was able to speak out confidently. She mentioned new groups and classes and asked the audience to watch out for her newspaper advertisement.

Afterwards, she saw Stella picking her way between chattering groups of women. 'Rosy, are you ready for 'the off'? I've had a good evening and caught up with old friends. Have you managed to see a few people?'

Rosy nodded and joined her in making their way to the exit.

The local paper was lying on the doormat when Rosy arrived home. She felt a twinge of excitement as she leafed through to find her own advertisement in print, but after flicking through it quickly, she sat down and went through the paper again, this time slowly. There was no advertisement for 'The Spotted Teapot'. That was a setback. She felt like crying. Her thoughts drifted straight to Jack; she wondered what he was doing now. She wished that her brother Alex were alive and then she thought of her parents over in Spain. She knew she was wallowing in self-pity. She'd make herself a hot chocolate and get lost in a good novel.

CHAPTER 8

Mandy agreed to watch over the tea shop for a few hours while Rosy met Tanya's bus in Taunton. Rosy realised how much she had been missing Tanya. On the drive home, Tanya filled her in on her busy life. She was looking forward to having some breathing space in the country.

'Y'know Rosy, you've been tied to it for so long. I'd quite enjoy watching over the "Spotted Teapot" on Saturday to give you a break. Have a day out. It'll be fun for me to try your job for a day.'

'It's tempting. But what if something came up?'

'I'm good with people so I'll be fine, as long as you keep your phone to hand, in case of emergencies.'

'It would be heaven to get away.'

'Okay and then we can have a girlie evening with a film on the TV and a bottle of red wine,' Tanya said.

They arrived to find the 'Spotted Teapot' full of weekend visitors. Mandy was looking on as twin toddlers hovered over a display of gingerbread men. Just like the twins, the biscuits were identical, but Mandy smiled patiently while they took their time to choose. Rosy shot a sympathetic look. After their mother had paid and taken them to settle into highchairs, Rosy introduced Tanya.

Tanya, office worker, and Mandy, artist, couldn't be more

different but they hit it off straight away.

'Now off you go and have your day out,' Tanya said, 'I'm happy here.' She beamed around all the customers.

'Thank you, I think I'll go for a drive and be a tourist for a change,' Rosy said.'I haven't looked around Wells for years. Is there anything you'd like me to bring you? There are a few bookshops there.'

Tanya said, 'I use an e-reader. But thanks. Get yourself a novel to curl up with.'

Rosy rummaged for the car keys in her pocket but came up with nothing. She tried the other pocket with the same result.

'I don't believe it.' She rushed out onto the drive to look through the car windows. The keys were on the floor of the hatchback. She must have dropped them there when she picked up Tanya's bags and then slammed the boot shut. She felt such a fool. She grimaced as she slunk back to Tanya. It just seemed to be the last straw.

She said, 'A good job Luke's renovated the bike. I've locked my car keys in the boot.'

Several customers took an interest as she explained what had happened. 'Oh dear, and you were all set to go,' the twins' mum said.

Rosy shrugged. A stylish looking man wearing a thin sweater with sleeves pushed up to his elbows was sitting in the corner nursing a large cappuccino. He hadn't ap-peared to take any notice of them and yet he leant forwards and offered, 'Is there anything I can do to help? Are any of the other doors unlocked?'

'Hmm, I don't know. I'll have a look.' Rosy went out to check. When she turned around, he was there on her heels. 'No, it's all locked. I'm completely stuck,' At least someone was interested but there was nothing anyone could do. 'I wonder if I should phone the breakdown service.'

He slowly circled the car. 'Ha, let me see if I can help.'

He produced a key ring with a set of metal probes. He flipped back a cover on the car door handle and bent down. With the tip of his tongue protruding, he carefully jiggled and turned first one and then another.

Rosy stood by quietly watching. She could hear someone cutting their lawn in the distance and closer to the 'Spotted Teapot' she could hear the throaty cooing of a woodpigeon.

He continued trying each metal tool until they heard a click. Then he stepped back grinning. 'Hey - done it.'

There came a terrible, undulating car alarm accompanied by rhythmic blasts of the car horn. Rosy covered her ears and retreated. The man dived onto the back seat, pushed the seatbacks down and knelt to reach into the rear boot area. He reappeared holding Rosy's keyring. He fumbled with it, finally shutting off the terrible racket, then held it aloft for her.

'Amazing,' Rosy let out a deep breath.

He smiled as he tossed his ring of metal tools against his palm. 'So, you can go and have your trip. I'm Ethan by the way, I've just moved here. Don't worry I'm not a car thief.' He grinned again.

'Well thank you, you saved me,' Rosy said.

She had almost abandoned her day out, but crawling along country roads in a traffic hold-up gave Rosy the space she needed to calm down. She wished that she hadn't reacted like a helpless maiden waiting to be rescued. She should have phoned the rescue service. 'I'll stay calm in the future,' she told herself.

Once she had parked in Wells and begun to stroll towards the centre, she glimpsed the striped awnings of a market. It was surrounded by medieval shops built of yellow stone. There was so much to look at. She was tempted by overflowing displays of trinkets in old bay windows, but the shops looked cramped inside, so she browsed the market stalls instead, breathing in the strong smell from the cheese stall and the perfumes from a candle seller. She could hear a busker who stood near an arched porchway, wearing a jester's outfit. She found herself matching her stride to the rhythm of his folk violin. Rosy walked through the arch into the Bishop's Palace Gardens. She wandered across sunlit lawns towards a moat and found a warm bench. Swans sailed decorously past while a clatter of ducks swooped down to land on the water. What a welcome respite from the claustrophobia of the village community.

Gradually the warmth of the sun and the low rushing of

water relaxed her muscles. The excited voice of a toddler disturbed her reverie. He had spotted the swans. When she turned away from the toddler and his family, she noticed a man with a familiar gait walking towards her. Surely it was Ken. They were so far from home that it seemed an unlikely encounter, but she felt a rush of pleasure at seeing him. She stood up and waved. He spotted her and quickened his pace.

'Amazing to see you here,' she said.

He sat down beside her. 'Well, I heard about all your problems with the car and thought you must be getting pretty stressed. I was worried about you. So, when they said you'd gone to Wells, I thought I'd come out here too.'

'We are lucky to find each other.'

'Well, it was a good bet that you'd visit the Bishop's Palace. It's such a beautiful setting. I imagine that you wouldn't want to spend time in any cafés. That would be too close to what you do every day at work.'

'I know.' She laughed. 'Although it's useful to check out other businesses.' She shifted around to face him. 'I'm touched that you came to look for me. I've really had no one "in my corner". So, thank you for having my back.'

'You are welcome my dear,' he said with mock pomposity, 'I'm only glad you don't think I'm stalking you.'

They sat in companionable silence. The slow-moving water encouraged people to slow to a meander as they strolled along the paths and crouched to feed ducks.

'This is relatively modern. Thirteenth century,' Ken mused.

'You remember all those facts and yet you're worried about losing your memory,' Rosy said.

'Ah yes, but once something's firmly lodged in my head it's there for good. The difficulty is with my short-term memory. Did I take my tablets? What time did we say we'd meet? Which students were due in my seminar? That is a worry.'

She grasped his hand. 'I know I've said it before, but please see a doctor. It may be the side effects of medication or . . . or anything. You seem to have decided that there's nothing you can do about it.'

His voice fell as he lowered his chin. 'Okay, you are right, I had accepted it instead of questioning. For you, my dear, I will go.'

Rosy laughed. 'Thank you and call me Rosy. When you say 'my dear' you sound about a hundred. How old are you anyway?'

He joined in with her laughter. 'Cheeky. I'm barely old enough to be your father. I suppose I play the role of the professor rather well. It ages me.'

They were visited by a pair of mallard ducks, the male with a glossy green head, accompanied by a drab brown female, but the ducks soon waddled away when they realised that there were no treats to be had.

'Do you want to walk around Wells Cathedral. It's impressive?' he said.

'You go if you want to. I'm luxuriating here in the sun.' She yawned behind her hand.

'I know. You deserve to. So, a customer called Ethan was your knight in shining armour. He was still chatting at the tea shop when I left.'

'Yes, it was lucky he knew what to do.'

'Wasn't it just. I spoke to him briefly. Interesting. . . I'm not sure what brought him to Sedgeborough. He's from Gloucestershire but that's all he said. I know parts of Gloucestershire, but he didn't seem to want to discuss it.' He narrowed his eyes in thought.

'You sound suspicious?'

'Hmm I have considerable experience of people, but my instincts may be off. If he stays around, I'll soon find out.'

'I suppose he could have some problem in his past – something that he's sensitive about.'

'Maybe,' Ken said.

Rosy wondered if Ken preferred to be the only useful male on hand, but then, she reasoned, there had never been rivalry between Ken and Luke.

She said, 'Well, I think he said he's staying in the village, but he'll probably have left the tea shop by now. You know, it's such a relaxed Saturday I'm in the holiday mood. We should do something enjoyable with the rest of the day. How about it, Ken?'

His face lit up. He glanced down at his watch. 'We could grab a snack in a country pub.'

Rosy took in a sharp breath. She had had a sudden consciousness of Tanya holding the fort back at the 'Spotted Teashop'. She bit her lip. She'd suggested something that she couldn't do.

'I'm so sorry. I forgot I must get back to see Tanya. She's only down for the weekend. We must do it another time.'

'Don't feel bad, but I will definitely hold you to that. A meal out in the evening would be an excellent idea.'

CHAPTER 9

Ethan was sprawling in the living room chatting to Tanya. They had kicked off their shoes and had a wine bottle and glasses on the coffee table. Their time for a girly chat was short as it was, but Rosy managed to hide her irritation. At least he had entertained Tanya while she was away.

Tanya beamed and waved her glass towards Rosy. 'Hiya, the café is all tidy. We had a good day. Just about every cake has gone.'

'Oh, that's great. Thanks.'

Ethan stood and shuffled around as though he were preparing to go, but Tanya said, 'We haven't eaten yet. Why don't you stay awhile, and we'll get a takeaway?'

It was an attractive proposition and even more tempting when Ethan offered pick it up from Langport.

After he'd set off, Rosy said, 'You two seem to be getting on well. I thought he'd be long gone by the time I arrived home. He's taken a shine to you.'

'No, I reckon he's keen on you. You never notice the signs.'

'That goes for both of us.' Rosy had no interest in men she had been burned too recently.

Ethan bought another bottle of wine to go with the food.

They spread everything out on the table and shared the dishes. The discussion turned to the experience of being a newcomer in Sedgeborough and Rosy told them about the women's business network. She explained that her newspaper advert had not materialised. She had phoned the newspaper afterwards and they hadn't been helpful. They claimed that it had been cancelled, but eventually agreed to offer a half price advert next time.

Tanya and Ethan were impressed with the way the tea shop had developed. Rosy flushed with pleasure. They were right, she had done well in the time that she'd been managing alone. Ethan was interested in the recycling projects. He said that he was excited by environmental issues.

'I don't have any skills in recycling, but I am quite a gardener. Maybe I could come along and help with the garden. It would be good to get involved in something while I'm here.'

Rosy reflected that everyone seemed extremely eager to get involved, while Tanya said, 'You don't work then?' She was always straight to the point.

'I'm a consultant for property developers so I keep an eye out for investment opportunities wherever I am,' he said. 'Where do you work Tanya?'

Tanya described her office. She confided that she was in difficulties at work. She and a co-worker had begun to see each other outside the office and now it was getting serious. She worried about the implications. For instance, if it didn't work out, they would have to continue to see each other as colleagues? She described the development of their relationship.

Rosy said, 'Sometimes you're too cautious for your own good. From what you say, this is a precious relationship and if it didn't work out – well one of you would have to look for another job. You're very employable.'

'Thank you. I've missed being able to chat with you.'

'I wish you could move down here,' Rosy said.

'I'm sure one day I'll get fed up with the city. I can see me marrying and settling in the country to have a family.'

Rather than being a comfort, Rosy felt a pang as she had lost hope of ever having her own cosy family life.

Rosy and Tanya spent some of the next day baking and after a short walk around the village, Rosy drove Tanya back to the bus station. Tanya tensed, her fist clenched, dreading the thought of Monday morning and having to try to act naturally in the office again.

As she left, Rosy said, 'Don't forget I'm at the end of the phone.'

Once alone again, Rosy planned to clean the tea shop from top to bottom before it opened on Monday morning. She cleared all the shelves and piled up display cases to be washed, but while she was mopping the floor, she spotted letters lying behind the front door. They must have arrived on Saturday. She stopped what she was doing to sit down at one of the tables. Official looking letters always sparked a twinge of dread. One had an embossed heading 'Fish, Barrington and Partners'. The letter said that Jack wanted to expedite the sale of the 'Spotted Teapot' so that each party could recoup their investment. It added that he would be open to offers to buy his share, subject to an independent valuation.

It wasn't a surprise, but Rosy was too dejected to continue mopping the floor. She felt attacked. She couldn't think logically. If only Tanya had still been here, she wouldn't have felt so alone. She pulled out her mobile to chat it through with her, but then realised that Tanya would still be sitting on a bus. Who had life experience and who would calm her? Her next thought was of Stella, but Ken would probably be the most level-headed. She decided to phone him.

Hello Ken, are you busy?

I'm not doing anything that can't wait. What is it, Rosy?

I've just opened a solicitor's letter about the tea shop. She opened her mouth to explain more, but he jumped in with, Don't let it worry you. Can you come over to the cottage? See you in ten minutes?

She let out her held breath, *Oh, okay, thanks.*

She finished the mopping, ran a brush through her hair and put the letter into her bag for him to read. As soon as she got out into the cool evening air, she felt calmer and had a prickle of anticipation at seeing Ken again.

Ken had set the cafetiere going ready to greet her.

'Mm - a welcome smell.' Rosy smiled.

'Have you eaten, my d . . . Rosy?' he corrected himself. 'I'm going to make some toast.'

Toast would be comforting. Ken placed the tray on a coffee table, collected his reading glasses and this time he sat beside her on the sofa. The previously spartan interior was more cheerful now that there was a small fire lit in the wood burner, there were rich throws over the back of chairs and a collection of large candles flickering on the windowsills.

He put on his glasses. 'I know anything official can feel like a threat. What do they say?' She produced the letter. He scanned it. 'Did you and Jack have a partnership agreement when you set up your business?'

'Yes, I think so. We're registered at Companies House and we signed masses of papers especially when we bought the old bakery from Stella's family.'

'Yes, a lot depends on what you originally agreed. I know it may feel threatening, but buying Jack out of the business might be the best course of action for you. Perhaps you could get a loan to do that? I think you should gather all your papers together and make an appointment to see your own solicitor.'

Rosy didn't want to hear this. She wanted him to say that

she could ignore the whole thing. Jack was supposed to have loved her, she a felt an ache under her ribs at the thought that it was now Jack causing her anguish.

'I know you're upset. You won't believe it now, but it will all work out. I don't think you'll have any problems in getting finance for the café. We've written a good business plan and you are building up regular customers.' He brushed her hand with his fingertips. She felt comfortable and relaxed all of a sudden. It was like coming home.

She bit into toast oozing with warm melted butter and jam, then smiled. 'Thank you, Ken. I always seem to be thanking you. I hope I can support you in the same way.'

'You already have. I arrived a stranger and now I feel part of a family.' His voice was warm and mellow. Rosy unconsciously laid her head on his shoulder. Just too late she realised what she'd done, but he seemed happy enough, so she made herself comfortable and watched the sputtering of the candle flame reflected on the wall.

What seemed like moments later Rosy became aware of the room again. There was a crick in her back and her feet were chilled. She felt the softness of Ken's pullover against her cheek.

'Ah you're awake,' he said. 'You must have needed the rest.'

Rosy sat up and finger- combed her curls. Ken slowly withdrew his arm, flexing it.

She said, 'Oh, I'm sorry. I didn't mean to sleep on you. Is

your arm all right?'

His eyes were dancing. 'My arm is honoured to be of assistance. It will wake up when its ready.'

'What am I like?' she said, echoing one of Tanya's favourite phrases. She could feel herself blushing. 'What time is it? I must get going. I've got to work in the morning and you – are you busy tomorrow?'

'Yes, I'm meeting a local archaeology company to share our knowledge.' He smiled. 'But before you go. . .' he moved in towards her with an intense look in his eyes. Rosy realised that Ken was about to kiss her. It was a surprise, but a welcome one. She closed her eyes. She sensed coffee and toast on his breath as his mouth drew near. His lips were apart, so she relaxed her own lips to meet him. He felt warm and soft. He pulled away and muttered, 'Rosy,' in a voice that she hardly recognised. More firmly than before, his lips brushed against her cheek and found her mouth again. Her heart quickened at this affirmation of feelings. She reached for his shoulders surrendering to her natural reactions.

As they drew apart, they continued to look into each other's eyes. He had deep brown eyes and dark brows. She felt a shiver.

He cleared his throat, 'I hope that was acceptable. I forget that, to you, I must seem an old man.'

Joy rose in her throat. She wanted to bubble with laughter. 'That was lovely. Thank you. And not such an old man – you're distinguished.'

She felt his shoulders vibrate in amusement. Rosy wondered whether he would stand up, offer his hand and lead her upstairs. No, it would be inappropriate. She was anxious to avoid an awkward moment, so she brushed his cheek with the back of her hand, 'So I really must be going Ken,' she said while injecting a tone of regret into her voice.

He offered to walk her home, but she declined. 'I haven't got far to go. See you soon.'

CHAPTER 10

The working week flew by. The art classes had been reasonably full, but two more classes were scheduled. Rosy needed to get some advertising out there. She decided she would chat with Ken about ways to advertise. She'd also managed to find the time to make an appointment to see a solicitor and contacted an estate agent for a valuation.

As he had promised, Ethan turned up to take a look at the garden. He picked some ripe apples and Rosy put them on one side to turn into Somerset Apple Cake.

Luke, who had been welding metal in the garage, came indoors for a break, so they stopped for coffee. He said that there would be another meeting of the Animal Rights Group that Thursday evening. That was the night that Rosy had a solicitor's appointment at 5pm, but she said she would be able to join them afterwards.

In quieter moments she pondered on the kiss with Ken. Neither of them seemed the smoochy type but she guessed it had happened because she'd felt vulnerable, and then cosy, in Ken's snug living room. He came into the tea shop on Wednesday to help with the baking. He seemed cheerful and acted as though nothing had happened. Her heart shrank, but it was probably for the best.

On Thursday Rosy dressed smartly to meet her solicitor. She felt like a child waiting outside the Head's office. Mrs

Crombie, the solicitor, might consider her a fool for getting into the partnership in the first place, but when they met, Rosy was pleased to hear that this was a common problem. Mrs Crombie had some simple solutions. Jack could dissolve their partnership, but all of the money raised from the sale of the tea shop would have to be used to pay off the mortgage and debts. That meant that there would very little left over to split between them. Surely it wouldn't be worth his trouble, unless he wanted to insist on selling up to be vindictive. Rosy was advised to investigate sources of finance to offer to buy him out.

It was troubling, but as Rosy had to drive to the Animal Rights meeting, she was able to put Jack to the back of her mind. There had been no food available at the last meeting, so she stopped off on the way for a ready-made sandwich. She could have kicked herself for not thinking to make one to bring along with her.

She didn't want to arrive at the group dressed for a solicitor's office. There was time to both eat the sandwich and make some changes. She took off the jacket and threw on a loose knit cotton sweater, then tossed her court shoes into the back of the car to replace them with a pair of trainers.

Arriving alone was an ordeal, but at least she knew some of the group now. Remembering its smell, she tried not to breathe in as she passed the Gents. She could already hear voices from the attic room. Most of the people there had been at the previous meeting apart from one stranger, a tall man with a thick, dark beard. Mandy and Luke were by the dartboard and she was surprised to see Ethan standing with them. They looked her way and Ethan raised his glass to her.

'So, they recruited you too,' she said to him, 'that was quick.'

Luke and Mandy had satisfied smiles. Ethan slapped Luke on the back. 'Yes this man can be very persuasive and it seemed like a good cause. So, we're both converts.'

Mandy leant towards her, 'Did you have a rush to get here?' but there was no time for further comment. Their leader started to speak and the woman beside him clapped her hands sharply.

'Hey everyone, I want you to meet our visitor. He's from a neighbouring group. It's Andrew, guys. A big welcome for Andrew.' He placed a hand on the bearded man's back and sat down.

They dutifully clapped and a younger man in glasses even gave a half-hearted 'Whoop.'

Andrew raised his hands to acknowledge them with a lopsided smile. 'Thank you guys. I'm here because we're planning a joint event. It's going to be a silent protest and non-violent – all the more powerful for that. We can rely on the graphic photographs in our leaflets to speak for us.'

'Good – 'bout time we took some action,' a grey-haired man in motorbike gear said. The others said little, but they had leant forward to listen and appeared interested.

Andrew added, 'It might not be for everyone. Only you can decide whether you'll come along. It's going to be next Saturday. We ask that those who attend dress completely in black. You won't need to say anything; the power is in your presence. If you want to cover your face with some kind of mask, that's okay too.'

Ethan nodded his head enthusiastically. 'Great. Where's it going to be?'

Rosy felt a jolt at his willingness to get involved immediately, while she still felt uneasy.

'We never divulge that at this stage.' Andrew addressed Ethan. 'We keep plans under wraps. But we'll provide transport: a minibus or sometimes we share cars. Don't worry about that.'

Rosy couldn't join in the Saturday action anyway as she would be busy at the tea shop. She stood back to see whether others were interested. Luke, Ethan and four others volunteered.

Mandy said sotto voce, 'I'm not going to leave you on your own on a Saturday. I'll help out at the tea shop.'

'Thanks, if you're sure,' Rosy said in a voice just above a whisper. She was grateful that Mandy was willing to put her first.

Afterwards, people sat around chatting. Opinion on animal rights would be divided in the Levels area, where farming was part of the economy. When Rosy stood to make her apologies, Ethan looked across from where he was perching on a stool.

'I'll get a lift back to Sedgeborough with you, if that's okay? I arrived with Luke and Mandy but if they don't have to drop me off, they can park the bus ready for the night.'

Rosy, taken aback at his sudden request, wondered why he hadn't brought his own car, but she remembered that he had rescued her car keys for her. She could hardly say no.

She had strewn personal items around the interior. He waited while she removed sandwich packaging from the passenger seat. He seemed to take up an inordinate amount of space so that she kept her elbows tucked in as she changed gear.

He said, 'I enjoyed the pizza night with you and Tanya. How is she?'

'She's back at work now. I haven't heard, but no doubt she'll come back to Sedgeborough again soon.'

'If you're lonely without her, remember I'm still here. This is the first time we've had a chance to have a one-to-one chat. It looks like we're into the same things,' he said.

'Oh, you mean animal rights.' Rosy knew very little about his interests.

'Yeh, I'm veggie already but I'm beginning to think about becoming vegan. It's really important right?'

'Err yes,' she said, thinking that the tea shop didn't stick to vegan ingredients. She concentrated on the driving while deciding how to explain her position.

'This was the second time that I've attended their meetings. Everyone has strong principles. I admire that.'

'Yeh - and I admire your work ethic. I hear that you haven't owned the 'Spotted Teapot' for long.'

Of course, Tanya would have filled him in on her recent problems. She hoped that they hadn't shared too much gossip. Ken had already noticed that Ethan was tight-lipped about his own background.

'That's right. So, tell me about yourself?' she said.

'Not much to tell really. I'm single and fancy free if that's what you were wondering.' Rosy wanted to deny that she was wondering, but the moment was gone as he went on. 'I love this area. The big skies, the birdlife. . . I'm an entrepreneur, so I'm looking out for business opportun-ities. Any start-up ideas or opportunities to invest with promising businesses.' He changed tack, 'I knew someone who worked at a factory farm. What he told me stirred my conscience and I'm vegetarian, so the group is ideal for me.'

She latched onto the mention of 'business opportunities' as she was looking for someone to invest in the tea shop. She told him about her business plan and the need for an investor. Disappointingly, he sat back and seemed to lose interest in further conversation. She hadn't asked for help outright, so she hoped she hadn't offended him.

'So, direct me to your house,' she said as they neared Sedgeborough.

'I'm at the other end of the village. Don't worry, drop me off at the Spotted Teapot and I'll walk the rest of the way.'

'No, it's no bother. It's just straight down the High Street, isn't it?' she said. They reached Townsend. He directed her to turn right into a 1970s housing estate. Each open plan front garden had a long drive with a selection of cars, large, small, old bangers, and caravans parked on it.

He indicated, 'I'm just here, thank you.'

There was a sleek, black car parked in his drive.

CHAPTER 11

Mandy shrieked. She had been helping tidy and restock the tea shop while it was empty. Her expression was alarming. She backed away from one of the cake displays, colliding with chairs behind her. She had dislodged a wicker tray of muffins on one of the lower shelves. Rosy blinked, hardly able to take in the situation.

'What?'

Then she spotted some movement. Standing completely still, Rosy saw rapidly squirming, white grubs swarming over icing and falling between the muffins. She couldn't make sense of it. Maggots? It was so unlikely.

Through gritted teeth, she said, 'Get a dustpan and brush.'

Mandy spun around and disappeared into the back.

Rosy stepped back, her chest heaving. She would have given anything to be elsewhere at that moment. She looked out of the window to check for witnesses. Sending Mandy for a brush wouldn't help. The whole thing should be taken as far from the tea shop as possible.

Rosy paused. She could do it – she would do it. Could she use cake tongs to pick up the box? No, they weren't strong enough to hold it. She opened the front door in readiness, screwed up her courage and grasped the edges of the box with both hands. Holding it awkwardly away from her body she manoeuvred between the tables and edged out of the door. She marched around the side of the building and then flung it onto the undergrowth in the back garden. The mass was still moving. A shiver prickled her arms. She shuddered.

Yet, it was still a peaceful country orchard scene – leaves waving slightly in the breeze. It was going to be a treat for the birds. In her wildest nightmares, Rosy could never have foreseen this. Surely it couldn't be a normal occurrence – so what had caused it? She wouldn't let anyone see her rattled. She strode back around to the front door. Mandy was standing holding a dustpan and brush and looking dazed.

Rosy dusted off her hands. 'We just need to brush around to make sure that nothing's fallen onto the floor or other shelves. I'm going to put up the 'Closed' sign while we make an assessment.'

Poor Mandy looked pale. Rosy placed a hand on her shoulder.

'Panic over. Sit down for a moment. I'm just going to wash my hands.' As she whisked away, irritation flashed towards Mandy. When this was all over, she'd sit down and work out what on earth had happened.

Rosy went to her bathroom to wash and then sat on the bed, every so often giving little shudders. She didn't think that Mandy had put the maggots there, so when had they been planted? It wouldn't be easy for anyone to leave maggots unobtrusively, unless they could get hold of fly eggs before the maggot stage. Who had had the opportunity? She hated to think that someone, that she saw as a friend, could sabotage her. So many people had been in and out of the tea shop. Was there anyone with a motive? Maybe a business that saw her as competition. Anyone who supported Jack could be against her. That could point to Manor Farm: Hyacinth and family and Stella. It was unimaginable.

That evening, she found herself turning the television right down to listen for noises outside. She made scrupulous checks on the tea shop each morning before opening. She watched her neighbours and paid closer attention to what customers were doing. Rosy acted naturally with Ken, Luke, Mandy, Stella and Ethan but she could feel herself pulling away from them too. At least no one had reported the incident to the local media, which would have been devastating.

Days later, Luke, Mandy and Ethan were chatting in the garage while Ken was baking in her kitchen. Rosy called everyone together for a coffee break. She brought up the incident of the maggots. It was clearly news to Ken, but she thought that the others had probably heard from Mandy. She appealed to them for help.

'It's upset me. I thought we were well liked here.' Then she remembered that Stella hadn't approved of New Age Travellers. She went on quickly, 'Anyway, can you think of anyone that might have planted the maggots here? Please keep an eye out.'

They were appalled by what had happened and were keen to support her; or at least that is how it appeared.

Days later an Environmental Health Officer called. Rosy

automatically checked that she was wearing her apron before going forward to greet her.

'Catherine Weston, good to meet you,' Catherine said shaking her hand. 'Nothing to worry about. I'm here to do one of our regular checks.'

Rosy was glad that Ken was around to take over, while she took the officer into the living room. Catherine Weston was only about her own age and had her hair scraped back into an elastic band. She had a friendly manner rather than being formal. Catherine wanted to see records of temperature checks and rotation of food. She was pleased to see that Rosy labelled everything with a use-by-date.

'You've probably realised, I didn't come here out of the blue. You'd be due to have a check at some point, but we had a warning that there had been maggots found here.'

Rosy felt a thud in her stomach. Only Mandy or the person who planted maggots could have reported them – and she didn't believe that it was Mandy. Catherine looked sympathetic, 'We occasionally have malicious reports, but you can probably understand, we have to investigate. And even when you are blameless, we need to help you work out how to avoid it.'

Rosy could feel herself flush. She hoped that, after the investigation, Catherine would be certain that they hadn't created the maggot problem. Catherine seemed satisfied. She spoke to Ken and pointed out that he should do a Food Hygiene Certificate.

'I'm so sorry. I should have thought,' Rosy was mortified.

Once Catherine was gone, Ken was concerned that his presence had caused her problems. Then he was amused that he would need to become a student for a change. He left early that day with the promise that he'd register with an online training company to take the certification test.

At closing time, Ethan hung back. When she went to bolt the front door, he followed her into the teashop. His unusual behaviour made her wary, so she was relieved when he explained.

'I'm gutted that you've had to deal with maggots. It's already a challenge to start a business without having incidents like that to deal with. Look, I've started successful businesses a few times now so if you need any advice just come to me. I know you're a tough cookie Rosy,' he said touching her wrist tenderly. 'Perhaps you'd like to come out for dinner with me? It would give you a break.'

His smile was disarming. He rivalled Jack in the looks department. Rosy felt flattered, but the idea of a date didn't appeal. Ethan hadn't let his guard down and so she wouldn't let down her own either – not yet anyway.

CHAPTER 12

Rosy was chatting with Mandy in the kitchen when they noticed Luke walk past the window.

Mandy knocked on the glass and waved him in. 'I didn't think you were coming down today?' she said.

'I needed to pick up a screwdriver.' He was still in blackened overalls, but he leant against the kitchen counter. He said, 'Did Mandy tell you how it went on Saturday?'

Rosy took a curious glance across at Mandy, 'No she hasn't given me any news.'

'Yeh he was wired when he came home,' Mandy said quickly.

Luke did seem to be buzzing. He said, 'You really felt that you were with likeminded people. We stood testimony to the cruelty shown to animals.'

'Was there much footfall in the town?'

'What people passing by you mean? Yeh it were crowded with Saturday shoppers n' most passers-by took a leaflet - you could see them glance down at it afterwards.' He nodded gravely. 'It will get to them in the end when they think about it.'

'I think you made a difference,' Rosy said. 'It was Ethan's first time. Was he okay?'

'Yeh he was sound.'

Rosy said, 'Well done to all of you.' She felt like a parent praising the children. Would she have gone with them if she hadn't been working? She still hadn't got to grips with the idea of turning the café exclusively vegan.

Luke and Mandy both went across to what was now his garage studio, and later when Rosy looked out of the window, Ethan had arrived and was standing chatting to them.

Rosy couldn't leave the tea shop to join them even though it was empty. Hyacinth, from the farm, walked past the front window. Rosy had been worried that the relation-ship with people at the farm had deteriorated, so she leant out of the door to call Hyacinth.

'Come on in, have a coffee. We've got some new upcycled metalwork and wall art.'

Hyacinth laughed. 'Oh, go on then anything for a skive. I shouldn't be out for too long though.'

She seemed to genuinely admire the tie-dyed wall hang-ings decorated with an array of beads. She stood with her head on one side. 'I'm tempted to buy one. Could you get one for me in tones of blue and purple?'

'I'll certainly ask Mandy,' Rosy said, writing a note on a pad. 'Not often I see you without the dogs?'

'No, they're happy to stay on the farm with whoever is working outside. They're missing the titbits that Stella brings in for them. She's been off ill for a week. I'd unlock the museum if anyone requested it but basically, she isn't around to oversee it.'

'Oh, I hadn't heard. Nothing serious I hope?'

'I'm not sure. I'm going to nip to see her in a moment.'

'Well send her my best wishes.' On impulse, Rosy reached for the tongs and put a couple of scones into a brown paper bag. 'There, take them with you. It might be all she fancies at the moment. And tell her I'll phone her for a chat soon.'

When Rosy and Jack were buying the building from Stella, Rosy had put Stella's number into the Contacts in her mobile. She waited until the café was quiet to slip into the kitchen.

'Hello, Rosy here. I hope I haven't woken you?

'No, no, I dozed this morning, but I am beginning to get better this afternoon. Thank you for the scones they were a treat.

'No problem. I bet you're feeling a bit low. Are you up to visitors? As long as it isn't catching, I could pop in tomorrow after the café closes?'

'Oh you make me quite emotional. I remember the times that I used to come to see all your family. It's just

*a heavy cold and I'll try not to sneeze on you. Yes, it'd be
lovely to have a visit, thank you.'*

*'Okay, until tomorrow then. I can hear the tea shop
doorbell going so I must dash.'*

She found Ken was there sprawling at one of the tables.

'Oh dear, what's wrong?' Rosy said, laughing.

He gestured around the room, 'I think I can afford to
slouch while there's no one else here. I'm sapped of energy. I trekked to the top of three barrows today. In fact,
I didn't stop for lunch.' Then he lowered his voice. 'And I
couldn't resist coming to see you again.'

He looked so drained that she wanted to go over to give
him a hug, but he was sitting in front of the window. It
wasn't a good idea. Rosy would like to let him know how
delighted she was to see him. She put it all into her tone of
voice. 'Oh Ken, I'm glad you came. Just relax while I act as
your devoted waitress. What can I get you?'

It was his turn to laugh. 'A tempting offer, but I can pull
myself around long enough to serve myself.' He stood up
and nipped behind the counter to operate the coffee machine. Rosy joined him to take a cup from the stack and
place it on a saucer for him. He turned quickly and put his
arm across her shoulders.

'You are a welcome sight,' he said and planted a kiss on
her forehead.

Rosy went warm all over and grabbed him around the

waist. 'We haven't been close since I came to see you. I'm glad you didn't regret kissing me.'

'Of course not.'

CHAPTER 13

Something plain like a quiche would suit an invalid. Rosy factored it into her baking schedule. She sailed through all the chores while, in her mind, thinking tenderly of Ken. She was glad, that he had turned to her when he was exhausted and sad, that he worried over his memory. He had had such a fascinating life. When she heard about his travels and his work, she realised how different they were. No bad thing though. There was more of him to know under each layer. She was curious about his past relationships, one day she'd steer the conversation that way.

She momentarily flushed when she heard knocking at the back door. She tore off her disposable gloves to dash to answer it. It was just Ethan and Luke dragging along a cast iron stove that Luke had picked up from a house clearance. He was planning to clean it up before deciding whether it would function again or whether to make it into a decorative item.

'Wondered if we could have a coffee before we start,' Luke said.

'Yeh, can you sort one out for yourselves,' she said before returning to her baking.

Rosy took a break once everything was in the oven. She hadn't realised that Ethan was still hanging around. 'Ah I thought you were in the garage.'

'No Mandy's joined Luke now and they're having a barney in there about future plans.'

'Um that's interesting. I thought they followed their whims rather than making plans.' She wondered whether the plans would affect her.

Ethan sat aside a chair turned back to front. He raised his eyebrows with a quizzical expression. 'Hey the Animal Rights group is going well, isn't it?'

'Yes, they seem a good crowd. You feel welcome when you're there, I mean,' Rosy said, wondering where this was going. Ethan was wearing a short-sleeved t-shirt. She noticed his strong arms flexed across the chair back.

He grinned, 'Yeh it was quite an experience going out with them. Andrew seems to be a leader.' He paused as though expecting her to add something about Andrew.

She said, 'From some other group, yes. I don't think the group here is particularly active. I've always felt that I ought to do something for a cause that I believe in, but, everything here seems super busy. Its hectic today and Ken hasn't been in to help with the baking. I'm taking some tea cakes 'n' stuff to Stella after we close. She's ill, you know.' Rosy wondered why she was suddenly babbling at him and gave a laugh.

Ethan joined her in laughing. 'Sorry, you're busy.' He looked at her from under his brows. He was definitely flirting. He got up as though to leave, but then perched on the edge of a table.

'About that. I felt for you when your advert was cancelled.

Someone's taking the proverbial. So, when I was in the pub, I got talking to a mate who works for the local paper. It's run by a tiny team. He said that he could actually remember the cancellation. He answered the phone. He could hear dogs barking in the background. It just happens it's so dead in there that he had a chance to scribble down the caller's number from the display, and it's someone who advertises frequently with them, Manor Farm.'

Without thinking Rosy let out a gasp, 'That's a bit sus.' It was virtually proof that someone at the farm had sabotaged her advert but also odd that anyone at the newspaper would take so much interest. Small towns for you.

Ethan grinned. 'More than a bit, I'd say.'

'So, it could have been one of Hyacinth's family or Stella. But why would they? I can't believe it.'

'Both Hyacinth and Stella have a motive,' Ethan said, 'their businesses are your competition.'

'Not really.' She smoothed down the neckline of her shirt. 'Neither of them runs a café. We complement each other. Except, well I suppose Stella said something about the people here not fitting with the "ladies who lunch". I don't know.' Rosy needed time to think about this.

'I'll keep digging if you like. Anything I can do to help you,' he said, meeting her eyes.

'Thank you.'

Rosy knew she should feel grateful, but now that Ethan had discussed her affairs in the pub, she would have to address the suspicion that she couldn't trust some of the people around her. The person who cancelled the advert was most likely behind the incident of the maggots in the café too. She didn't want to believe that it was Hyacinth or Stella. Stella had been a family friend for so long.

Of course, Jack always lurked at the back of her mind. But she didn't even think that he was still in the village. He should surely be trying to make amends for all that he had put her through rather than making trouble – but it's surprising how people can convince themselves that they are not at fault. So, she ought to put him somewhere on the list of suspects. Part of her even suspected Ethan. Could she believe what he told her? It was strange the way he became involved with her so quickly. She was probably discomfited by him because of his model-like good looks. He seemed to be trying to cast himself as a hero.

Ethan was looking out of the window at her vintage bicycle now displayed without the launch day garlands. She longed to get on that bike and escape far away, speeding down hills with her hair flying out behind her.

She should give herself a good shake. 'Thank you for being concerned, but no don't keep digging,' she said, 'I'm going to make some discreet enquiries of my own. You're right, I shouldn't have put it behind me. It was self-preservation – I'm afraid I close my eyes to unpleasantness and that's not useful.'

He swallowed. 'Okay,' he said slowly, 'tell you what, I haven't been to the Country Life Museum or the garden centre at the farm, if you get someone to look after the tea shop we could go together. You could take the chance to look around and you need a break from here.'

She had been right. He was keen to be involved. She smiled at him. 'Thank you I'll bear it in mind. It's closed at the moment, as Stella's off ill, so we had better leave it a while.'

* * *

Stella had taken on her family's semi-detached house after her parents' death. It was in a cul-de-sac surrounded by the low fields of the Somerset Levels. Each house had a long lawn to the front. Stella had enhanced her's with pots of annuals and hanging baskets. The moment Rosy knocked, the front door flew open. Stella must have been standing behind it.

She immediately returned to the living room and lay on the settee. She was surrounded by magazines and used mugs. An open book lay on the floor beside her. Rosy showed her tea cakes in a paper bag and the boxed quiche.

'I'll take them into the kitchen for you, shall I? And don't get up. I'll get you another drink and get myself one.'

Stella held the back of her hand to her forehead dramatically. 'Thank you you're a star.'

Despite her illness, she had applied make-up and styled her hair. Surely, she should be back at work soon. She must be getting bored at home. Stella recounted the plot of a film that she'd just seen. Eventually, she asked, 'So how's your little café going?'

'It's steady. Busy afternoons but quieter in the mornings. I'm glad of the time to try out different recipes.'

'I thought Ken did all of that.'

'Oh no, Ken's working on his own research project. He drops in to bake, because it's therapeutic and he enjoys the company I think,' Rosy said.

'I can see that. It would be too quiet for me in the museum if I weren't connected to the farm. I'm really missing those dogs,' Stella said.

'Mm I need to drum up business. Get more advertising out there. I had planned one for the local paper you know,' Rosy said, taking a sip of tea and watching Stella, 'but someone phoned to cancel it.'

Stella's face stayed blank, but there was a split-second flicker in her eyes, before she rallied to say, 'Well, that's nuts. Who'd do such a thing?' After a pause she added, 'So tell me, are your weird visitors still at the café?'

Rosy felt her jaw tighten, 'You make it sound like I have ghosts. Yes, Luke and Mandy are an amazing help. They do some of their own stuff, but they help a lot too. They aren't weird, it's just their style.'

'Each to their own.'

Stella seemed to have mentioned them as a change of subject or even as a hint that she thought they were guilty. It made Stella seem a more likely culprit.

'Stella, we've known each other for ages. I just wondered whether everything's cool between us? When Jack moved into the farm it put you in a difficult position. I've been wondering though, I hope I hadn't already offended you when you weren't invited to the wedding. It was such a small venue we couldn't invite all the people we'd have liked.'

'No, no don't be silly,' Stella said, 'I don't take sides between you and Jack.' Her eyes turned to look at the fake-log gas fire.

'Well, I felt that there was something and I'd like to clear the air if there is.'

Stella drew in a breath, 'Okay, if you must know. It was hard for me to say goodbye to the old bakehouse, even though my family didn't make a go it – or maybe because we didn't make a go of it. Don't get me wrong, we were also pleased when you and Jack bought it. I mean, my parents' health was failing even then, so it helped financially, but'. . . she pursed her lips, 'I hadn't realised that we'd left the painting of Sedgeborough in the attic. It's been in my family a long time. My father was happy when he bought it. He always believed that it was worth more than he paid for it. Then there it was, on the wall of the tea shop.'

She seemed to fold in on herself and shot a sideways look at Rosy. 'You probably think that you own it, but you know, it was left by mistake.'

Rosy went cold, 'I wish you'd said something. I had no idea. It was covered in cobwebs and dust when we found it.'

'But would you have just given it to me? No!'

Now Rosy was certain that Stella had sabotaged the business. She felt breathless. 'You could have asked. I might have given it to you, and I deserved to know that you had a problem.' She thought of the times that Stella had been their babysitter and tears sprang to her eyes, 'You cancelled my advert, didn't you?'

Stella clenched her jaw but said no more.

Rosy continued, 'And you put foul things into my muffin display.'

'What, no I wouldn't do that.' Stella shook her head violently. 'If you're going to start accusing me of everything that comes into your head, you can just go.' She swung her legs down to sit upright. 'You've come here acting the successful businesswoman visiting the sick, but you don't fool me.'

'We need to get on together as we're in the same village, let's see if we can come to some sort of compromise.'

'Yes, that would suit you wouldn't it. Everything comes to you so easily, well not this time it doesn't.'

Rosy was shocked by the sudden change in tone, 'I'm sorry if I've upset you. I'm going to leave now. I'm sure we can sort it out sometime.'

Stella just looked toward the door. Rosy couldn't believe that a family friend could turn on her so suddenly, she fought back tears, gathered herself together and stood up.

'Well, goodbye.'

Stella pursed her lips. Rosy was left to let herself out of the front door. She believed that she had found her saboteur and now she knew the motive. Her arms and legs were shaky. She immediately started the car, anxious to drive away as soon as possible, but after turning the corner onto the main road she drew up to the curb and pulled on the handbrake.

The familiar village, with memories of her childhood, didn't feel so cosy after all. Rosy held onto the steering wheel and laid her forehead on it. She had been proud of the way she faced obstacles but finally she had reached the limit. She didn't even want to see the the 'Spotted Tea Pot' at the moment – she had an irrational fear that something awful would appear there. She should let Ethan know that he had been right and thank him again.

CHAPTER 14

Rosy feeling wobbly, couldn't think clearly. Ethan's black car was still on the drive, so he was probably in. The weak light of the sun cast a deep, rosy light over the house walls. The air was cooling. She grabbed a cardigan from the backseat of her car and strode up the front path to knock. There were no sounds from inside. Even though there was no one to see her, she felt foolish to be left standing on the doorstep. This time she knocked harder and for longer. It became imperative to discuss the Stella situation with him as soon as she could.

She could hop across the lawn to peek through the front window, but if she were spotted, it would make her look desperate. Just as she was about to turn to leave, she heard someone approaching the door. Ethan opened it and stepped to one side to admit her. He was unflustered, yet all he wore was a bath towel.

Rosy backed away. 'Oh no. I'm so sorry. I didn't mean to disturb you.'

He waved her in. 'Come on. I don't want to stand here dressed like this. Come in.'

She hesitated. 'No I couldn't.'

Ethan put a bare foot onto the path and grasped her by the wrist. 'You must have wanted me for something. Follow me.'

It was easier to step inside than create drama. She followed him, observing the way his muscles moved under the towel as he walked. She was glad the waistband was firmly turned over.

'Sit down. Don't be nervous.' He pulled the front window curtains closed, then flung himself down in a chair opposite the sofa. Rosy was transfixed by his hirsute legs, muscular arms, chest and shoulders. She forced herself to look away.

'So, what's wrong? Tell me all about it,' he said.

'Seeing you with damp hair and dressed in a towel has shocked me out of a panic.' She giggled and then gave in to laughter.

He laughed too. 'I didn't realise you were so easily shocked.' He moved across to sit beside her. 'But tell me why you were panicking?'

'You were right about Stella. I don't know whether Hyacinth was in on it too, but I confronted Stella and I could see guilt in her eyes. She told me that she resented me over the sale of the building and particularly that I'd got a painting that she thought was hers – it's an obvious motive. She was pretty foul actually.'

He shook his head grimly. 'No need to panic though sweetie, now that you know your enemies you can deal with them.'

She shrivelled inside. 'It's horrible knowing that someone can plot against me like that. It makes me feel sick. I'm getting paranoid.'

'Who can blame you.' He moved closer to stroke her hair. 'She's just a lonely woman nursing bitterness. You're a fighter, you know?'

She found herself breathing rapidly. 'I don't feel like one. I can't cope.'

'Take deep breaths. Now breathe with me. One,' he said, taking a deep breath, and then slowly, 'two three, four, five, on the outbreath. Come on count with me.'

Rosy joined him. It did help. Breathing in unison was like becoming one being, and yet how bizarre it was to be sitting beside a half-naked man doing relaxation exercises.

'How did we get to this? I must be going. Thank you for helping,' she said.

'Don't go yet. It's barely gone 9 o'clock. Stay and have a drink with me.'

Rosy took another deep breath. She was too emotionally drained to be able to make any decision.

'I'll just be a minute,' he rose to leave. She wondered whether his towel was going to fall open. It swung slightly but stayed in place. He returned with two full glasses. 'Isn't it lucky that I've got champagne in the house. We deserve to toast our detective skills.'

But they weren't really in a jubilant mood. They sipped gently. Rosy savoured the dry fizz on her tongue. Maybe she'd been getting strung up about nothing. At least now she had insight into Stella's problem. She decided that she'd send Stella a text offering to get the painting valued, then they could decide what to do about it. If she sent it to auction, she could share the profit with Stella. Maybe that would help.

She told Ethan her idea.

He said, 'Yes, that'll work if it's about the money and not about sentimental value.'

'Oh, I think it is about the money.'

'Can I help you forget her,' he said in a low voice leaning in for a kiss. She felt a lurch of lust as she held onto his biceps and tasted champagne on his lips. Kissing him was like drowning in mead. Eventually he drew away, took her glass and placed it with his own on a coffee table. He caught her hand, 'Come on?' she followed him up the stairs and into a bedroom.

Rosy took a moment to think, 'Is this what I want?', he wasn't pulling her, but tenderly leading her forward. He had let himself be vulnerable – undressed and bare foot. She let him lower her onto the bed and take up where they'd left off downstairs. She could sink into the bed and never get up. They wrapped themselves around each other so that his towel fell away. He undid the top button of her blouse then she took over to unbutton the rest. The close connection with Ethan soothed her anxiety.

* * *

When she awoke the warm sense of wellbeing had gone. His gentle snores sounded loud in her ear. The quilt had

ROSY'S RECYCLING TEA SHOP

become entangled around her legs and its cotton was rough against her arm. She opened one eye; everything was unfamiliar. A digital clock said 4 am. She would disturb Ethan if she got up to leave, so she resolved to go back to sleep and deal with everything in the morning. Rosy was naked. She missed the comfort of night clothes against her skin. She hoped that he would give her privacy to collect her clothes and dress in the morning.

She was glad that she still had a good opinion of him. He was a gentle and caring man with a touch of wildness around the edges and he'd worked hard to win her trust by helping to track down her saboteur. But despite that, she still didn't know him. They'd missed the stage where you find out what you both feel about life and spend hours having heart to hearts. She and Ken had been through that stage. What about Ken? He would be hurt if he learned that she'd slept with Ethan. Should she keep it from him? If she did that, there would always be something unspoken between them. It made her head hurt to think about it. The digital clock now said 4:50 she must try to relax. Ethan turned over in his sleep and she took the opportunity to change position without disturbing him.

The next morning, Rosy awoke alone in Ethan's bed. She dressed in record time. She could hear movement downstairs. He was in the kitchen. 'Hi Ethan,' she called.

He popped his head out of the kitchen door. 'Ah you're awake sweetie. Did you sleep well?'

'I must have done. I feel rested but I'm anxious to get back to prepare the tea shop for opening.'

'Surely you have time for some breakfast?'

He looked crestfallen. It was awkward, but if she didn't get home quickly it might be awkward there too.

'I'm sorry,' she said, making sure to inject regret into her voice. 'Thank you for . . . everything. But I can't stop.'

He shot across the room and folded her in his arms, 'Take care then, I'll see you later.' She felt his kiss brush her cheek. She smiled and returned it then dashed away.

CHAPTER 15

Back home, Rosy was thankful for the empty silence of the early morning house. She raced upstairs for a shower and a change of clothing. She had lied to Ethan about being rested and she would dearly like to fall into her own bed and sleep for the rest of the day, but life goes on.

She remembered the decision to message Stella.

Hi Stella

I hope you are feeling better. I don't want bad feeling between us. I am going to get the painting valued and then if we sell it, we can share the proceeds. Rosy xx

She hoped that would appease Stella. It seemed a fair solution. To restart her day, she opened the front door and stepped outside. Sedgeborough High Street was just as it had always been, only Rosy felt different. If her adventure of the night before had achieved nothing else, it had made her feel like a desirable woman again.

The shape of the bushes behind the dry-stone wall opposite patterned shadows across the road. Her old bicycle on the cobbled frontage made her wistful about the past. Rosy could imagine she had been part of Sedgeborough since the old days of the painting. She breathed deeply of the fresh air, tinged with faint farmyard smells. A drop of moisture landed on her bare arm. It hadn't rained for a while, so rain would be welcome. She held out a hand. It was that fine rain that quickly soaks.

Her thoughts were interrupted by the telephone. Could Stella be responding to her text so quickly or maybe Ethan couldn't live without her? It was Ken. He apologised for not seeing her in the last few days. He had been travelling. Even though he had plans for today, he wanted to pop in first to bring news on the advertising front.

'Yes of course. Come round,' she said, despite now feeling mortified about her night with Ethan. She was sure Ken didn't see her as that type of person, but yesterday she hadn't been thinking properly. It had been flattering. She guessed, subconsciously, it could have been a way to get her own back on Jack. Stupid really, she wasn't planning to tell Jack about it. Everything was all mixed up.

Ken arrived at the tea shop and scuffled his feet on the door mat. She had seen him scruffy and muddy; she had seen him sharply dressed, now he was wearing a mustard-coloured waistcoat with a checked shirt and cravat. Did the man change with the clothes?

'I hope you don't think that I've been neglecting you. I have some news I'd like to discuss.' He sat down crossing his legs at the ankle. 'I've been asked to speak on my research on barrows on local radio, so I mentioned that I was involved in a fascinating café in which the proprietor sells upcycled objects. They were keen for you to do an interview. So, free publicity. You can't beat it.' He pulled a business card out of his waistcoat pocket. 'Here's the number, call Mike and arrange a time to go in.'

'That's awesome. I hope I can find enough to say,' she said.

'I'm sure you will be able to describe some of the more outlandish objects, and the craft classes. You'll be able to tell a few little stories.' He smiled. 'I've got the greatest confidence in you.'

Rosy was reminded how pleasant it was to collaborate with him. She tapped the card and put it in her apron pocket. It made her feel even worse. She wanted to hide her face, so she spun her back to him as though to work behind the counter.

She said, 'I'll get on to it today, thanks. Have you got time for a drink, or do you need to get to your appointment?'

'No time really. I'll come in tomorrow and do some baking for you.'

'That's a deal.'

Ken's good nature made it difficult to drive away her guilty feelings. She would take the Ethan experience and bundle it into a cupboard right at the back of her mind. Ken was even apologising. 'I'm sorry I haven't been around more often. I know you felt a bit wobbly after the maggot incident.'

'Shh,' she said laughing. 'Yes, I did feel that way, but you give me a lot of time out of your schedule and I'm grateful. I think we've solved the mystery of who planted them here.'

'Really.' He sat forwards chin on his hand. 'Now this is worth being late for my appointment. What did you find out?'

'Ethan met one of the newspaper staff in the pub. His contact was interested enough to recognise Manor Farm's phone number on the caller display when my advertisement was cancelled. Amazing really, apparently Manor Farm phone the paper regularly to place adverts – and he heard dogs barking in the background. You wouldn't believe, would you, that they have so few calls that they remember individual ones?'

'Hmm' he shrugged, 'it's a small paper but . . .'

'Oh yes and then I went sick visiting to Stella.' She gave him her perception of that meeting.

'It sounds as though you're right. Now you can watch Stella in case she does anything else suspicious and now you've found a solution to the problem of the painting you might be able to mend bridges. An excellent outcome. But, so, this was initiated by Ethan. . .' He frowned.

Rosy couldn't meet his eyes. 'Well, he was helpful. You just don't like him, do you?'

'No, I apologise if I am wrong, but I have an instinct about him and I question his motives.'

Rosy hoped that she hadn't flushed or looked guilty. Ken was endearing when he was concerned.

'I do appreciate that you're looking out for me, but don't worry I'm a big girl really.'

He stood up and gave her a reassuring touch on the shoulder. 'Okay, duly noted. Maybe I see him as a rival. But we'll have to discuss it another time, I'm afraid I really do have to go now.'

She stood on tiptoes to kiss his cheek. He misunderstood the movement and turned to face her, so that her peck landed awkwardly on his mouth. She laughed as he wiped his mouth with the back of his hand.

She waved as he drove away. 'See you tomorrow, Ken.'

CHAPTER 16

Ken couldn't get thoughts of Ethan, and of the new information about Stella, out of his mind. Ethan couldn't be as altruistic as he presented himself. Rosy was still vulnerable after her problems with Jack. Ken wanted to protect her. He had an image of Rosy holed up in the fortress Spotted Teapot, wondering who her friends were. When he met Stella at the Rural Life Museum, she had seemed a nice woman. He would be disappointed if it really were Stella who'd planted maggots.

She needed him in her corner. When he next called into the tea shop after work he said, 'It's been a long day. I don't feel like cooking. Would you like to accompany me to a restaurant? I'd be honoured if you could, that is, if it isn't too short notice.'

'You must be tired, are you sure? We could get a take-away instead,' Rosy said.

He sounded buoyant. 'I'm sure I'll be fine after a shower and a coffee. I'm not a senior citizen you know.'

The day spent serving customers had been exhausting but Rosy only needed a short rest, possibly with a foot soak, and she would be able to enjoy a meal out.

Hours later, the crunch of gravel heralded the arrival of Ken's classic Rover. This version of Ken was an upgraded one. Rosy couldn't work out exactly what he'd done but he was slicker, sharper. She smiled at how pleased with himself he looked. While she locked the building, he sped around to the passenger door to hold it open for her. She felt a bubble of amusement, but she appreciated his chivalry.

They fell into familiar conversations as they drove. As they neared a well-known restaurant located in a former stately home, Rosy wondered if she had dressed smartly enough, but they drove past it and on to a major road. It seemed a long journey.

'Hmm I'm super hungry. How about you?' she said.

'Yes, I feel ready to eat. Don't worry it isn't far now. I didn't know the restaurants around Sedgeborough, so I'm heading to my old haunts. We'll drive past the university and I'll show you the department I work in.'

Grey clouds brought an early dusk. Lit windows glowed in the town. They drove past a concrete bus station and the rear of a supermarket. Then he pointed, 'There it is! On the corner of the building there. That's my office window.'

She craned her neck to see. 'Do you miss being in the uni?'

'No, not entirely. Being out in the field lets me immerse myself in the research.' They pulled to a halt and he again nipped around to open the passenger door. Ken took Rosy's arm as they entered an opulent Chinese restaurant. The vast space, suffused in spicy aroma, was filled with red velvet upholstery, red-tasselled lampshades and Chinese gilt wall decorations. Once at the table, the waiter took their drinks order and left them to read their menus.

They started with a glutinous, deeply flavoured soup sipped from porcelain spoons. Ken told Rosy of his own travels in China. The next course arrived still loudly hissing and fizzing on hot cast iron. Once Rosy had torn open the packet of chopsticks she felt obliged to try them, but each time she trapped a morsel it fell back onto the plate. She pulled a face at Ken and tried skewering the meat instead. He laughed and said, 'You've managed to get some on your nose already. If we were in more informal surroundings I'd come nearer to help. Watch me.' He demonstrated the chopstick hold.

Then he cleared his throat ostentatiously. 'Now for my news.' He noticed she was looking apprehensive. 'Don't worry it's extremely good. I took your advice and went to the doctor. I paid to go privately to speed up the testing process. It's official – my memory problems were caused by stress. I'm so relieved that I'm not on an inexorable slide into dementia. I couldn't imagine being able to continue to work or imagine any future. Now I can.' He gave her a broad smile, his eyes sparkling.

'It sounds as though work must have been quite stressful though. How can you reduce stress?' she said.

'I know, I need to work out whether it's the particular team I'm in or whether I need a complete change of career. But the important point is that now I've got my future back I feel free to pursue a relationship with you. If you feel the same way that is.'

Rosy sat back to take it in. He had delivered this as a momentous piece of news, almost like a proposal of marriage. Heat radiated in her chest and ran down her spine.

She had felt a close affinity with Jack, but Ken shone out as a cross between her guardian angel and someone that she could admire for his knowledge. She considered anew Ken's dark eyebrows over deep set eyes, his grey flecked hair and his familiar long chin.

He was hoping for an answer, and the memory of her night with Ethan made her hesitate. A few days ago, a man so contrary to Jack's type would have seemed like the answer, but now she wondered whether she could trust her own judgement. How had she so easily fallen for Ethan?

'Ken, I'm sorry that I can't tell you how I feel yet. I think there's chemistry between us, but my emotions are still in a turmoil over Jack. I don't trust myself to make choices anymore.' He looked aghast so she hurried on, 'I really like you, and recently I've come to rely on you as a close friend, but, well, I didn't know that we were heading down the dating route.' He was looking troubled, and she was at a loss as to how to handle the conversation. She would just be honest. 'Okay, I just think, I need to let you know about the other night.'

'I'm sorry, what's all this about?'

'Please don't judge me. I'm not myself.' He was looking wary, so she decided to get it over with. 'I was distraught after visiting Stella and well, Ethan had been discussing Stella with me just before then, so I turned to Ethan. I was feeling lost and in a bit of a state. Um, we spent the night together.'

'You went to his house?'

She nodded.

'Rather than mine.' There was silence between them apart from the sound of his breathing. Ken picked a at non-existent speck on the tablecloth. 'You didn't have to admit it. I appreciate your honesty, but I can't pretend that it doesn't mean anything to me.'

Rosy's chest tightened and she felt hot. This could ruin everything. 'I'm sorry, it was stupid. I certainly don't plan to do it again, but it has made me realise that I'm all over the place emotionally.'

At that moment their server brought little cups of coffee. They stopped speaking. Rosy had the urge to rush to the loo.

Despite his stricken expression, Ken reached across to take her hand. 'I'm sorry. I don't know what to say. I'm naturally disappointed.' She was hurt by the sadness in his eyes. 'I had no idea.' He stroked her thumb urgently. 'I'm glad that you can be so open with me and I really hope it won't come between us.'

All this emotion made Rosy's limbs feel heavy and her eyes sting. She forced a smile. 'I only wish I could just say yes let's make a go of it, but it wouldn't be right. Can we be friends, at least for now?'

She would hate to lose Ken's affection, so she felt a pang when, he immediately replied, 'Yes, I think that's a sensible suggestion. You look tired.' He gave a weary smile. 'Shall we finish these coffees and go back to the car?'

They were quiet on the way home. Ken glanced across

'Tired?'

'Mmm, I can't even. . .'

'Close your eyes then while I drive.'

She was comfortable enough in his presence to close her eyes. She dreaded arriving home and the moment of saying goodbye. She might have kissed him but now everything was different. Rosy felt mortified. She wished Ken's declaration unsaid and then she wouldn't have felt any need to tell him about Ethan. Ken turned off the engine, undid his seat belt and sat for a moment gazing down the street. She suddenly felt irritated and unwilling to deal with his disapproval.

'Well thank you for taking me out,' she said breezily. 'We both need a good night's sleep.'

'Of course, my dear. See you soon,' he said.

As she left the car, she felt a sharp pang. It was like the end of her relationship with Jack all over again.

CHAPTER 17

On Sunday morning, Ken went through the motions of preparing Earl Grey tea and fig jam on oatcakes, but Ethan was on his mind. Rosy had obviously ignored his warnings about Ethan. He hadn't noticed them growing closer. He didn't want to blame her. Despite her occasional misguided decisions, she was an admirable person. He had felt melancholy when he arrived in Sedgeborough, but she made him feel alive again. If he could get past the image of her with Ethan, he would love to begin a gradual courtship. Ethan was all surface charm and Ken hoped to find a way to show that to Rosy.

He cleared away and sat down to the laptop. He had no idea of Ethan's surname and couldn't think who would know it. Searching under Ethan's Sedgeborough address didn't yield results because Ethan had only just begun to rent it.

He said he'd moved from Gloucestershire. Ken searched Facebook profiles for people called Ethan in Gloucestershire. Many didn't include photographs, so he couldn't know whether he'd found the right Ethan. Finally, he made a search under property developers and found a website for 'Ethan Baker – contact us for a consultation on your property. Can't sell your property? Give us a call?'

Ken lost hope at that point. It could prove Ethan's backstory. He carried on searching, this time under Ethan Baker. There was surprisingly little further online evidence for him even on the electoral roll. 'Inconclusive,' he decided. Was he crazy to do this?

The following day, Ken drove to Gloucestershire to check out the address on Ethan Baker's website. Once he left the motorway, he pulled in to set map guidance on his phone. This little adventure was raising his spirits. Eventually, he was directed into a side road past a row of garages. The correct address was a series of single storey buildings and storage sheds arranged across a concrete parking area. It looked too large for a small property developer's office but maybe there were multiple businesses.

He got out and scouted around the building looking at the signage. Beside a rough painted door was a sign, 'E. Smith builders', he leant on the door but it was locked. At the other side of the building was a sign, 'Advanced processes – plastics and aluminium sidings'. He thought it strange that there was so little going on, considering that all these businesses must have had to pay rent to use the premises. He was beginning to consider leaving when he heard the rattle of a metal padlock on a door. There must be someone around after all. A heavily-built, shaven headed man stood, legs planted firmly. Ken read the sign beside him, 'K & F Mixed Martial Arts'. That made sense.

The man with the shiny head looked quizzical but said nothing. Ken moved some way closer. 'Can you help me? I'm looking for a property consultant listed at this address, Ethan Baker.'

'No, there's a builders' office here, but I don't know that name.'

The hunch had paid off. There was no Ethan Baker at the address given on the website. Ken still wasn't sure that he had enough information to question Ethan and to show Rosy. If Ethan had his wits about him, he'd be able to bluster his way out of it and make Ken look like a crazy stalker. Was Ethan the person who had deposited the maggots? Ken brooded all the way home.

It was dusk when he re-entered Sedgeborough. The road in front of his cottage was parked up. He drove on to where it widened beside the church and pulled in beneath overhanging trees. He was so deep in thought that he hardly noticed bats flittering around the trees and a cat that stopped to watch him. Ken concluded that the only solution was to keep Ethan under surveillance.

CHAPTER 18

Andrew, the speaker from the Animal Rights group, turned up at the Spotted Teapot. Rosy spotted him when he was standing in the drive talking to Luke. They looked up when they saw Rosy appear. Andrew nodded unsmilingly and said, 'Hey,' either in greeting or as a goodbye, and strode away.

'Bye mate,' Luke called.

Rosy said, 'That's Andrew, isn't it?'

Luke leant his shoulders against the rough cottage wall and took out a roll-up paper and tobacco.

'Yeh, he came to warn me. You ought to know too. Some of the group want to do something heavy, like sabotaging an animal testing centre, know what I mean? It's too much.' He licked along the paper. 'Anyway, Andrew turned up to tell me that there's been a cop asking around. So, there must have been a leak somewhere.' He shrugged. 'I've no idea where but I don't need that shit. I guess it's time for us to move the bus on.'

'What leave Sedgeborough?'

'Yeh, it was good here - cool. We might hole up somewhere ready for the winter.'

It was another sack of problems added onto her shoulders. Rosy willed herself to stay steadfast in the face of yet more doubts about the trustworthiness of her circle. It would mean that she'd lose Mandy's help.

'I'd hate to see you go. If we aren't directly involved in anything criminal, it shouldn't be a problem, should it?'

'Trouble follows us, so I just keep moving.' He looked at her and his voice softened. 'Maybe we'll come back this way next summer.'

Rosy was under so much pressure that she'd started to forget things. She forgot to pick up yeast and icing sugar at the cash and carry. Mandy was now a paid member of staff. At least, while she was still there to fill in, Rosy could nip to the supermarket.

It was a surprisingly novel experience to use the supermarket car park and to mingle with other customers. No time to browse though, Rosy scanned the overhead signs to find the baking supplies. She got a warm feeling when a couple of 'Spotted Teapot' customers greeted her and then when she realised that she recognised the woman at the till. Her face shape and slightly protruding teeth were so familiar.

'I'm sure I know you. Is it Janice Harker?' she said.

The woman looked at her blankly and then burst into a smile. 'Of course, we went to school together. Well, I never. You had your hair in an Alice band when I last saw you.'

'And yours was a different colour.' Rosy laughed.

'And now I'm Jan Jones. Are you back here on a visit?' Janice looked back at the till and rang up the total.

'No, I run 'The Spotted Teapot' in Sedgeborough. You must come in sometime.' Rosy said, suddenly distracted by a customer at one of the other tills. She could only see the back of the woman's head, but she seemed familiar.

'I might just do that,' Jan was saying. Rosy gave her a smile, before her eyes darted back to the woman with the sleek, blond hairstyle. It looked just like Stella. She would rather hang back than risk meeting up with Stella here. They hadn't seen each other since the awkward meeting at Stella's house.

She couldn't stay at the check-out indefinitely. The customer behind nudged her in the thigh with a trolley. So now, Rosy was inadvertently walking to the exit in parallel with Stella. Stella twisted in her direction and gave a pinched smile. 'Hello, this is a coincidence.'

'Yes, it is. I'd wanted to talk to you, but maybe not here.'

Stella paused to push her hair behind her ear. 'Of course, we ought to talk sometime. After all, we live in a small village and we're neighbours.' She turned as though to leave. 'My car's over here.'

On impulse, Rosy reached out for Stella's elbow. 'The picture's been valued now. I think you'll be interested in the results. Have you got some time? We could sit on the grassy bank at the edge of the car park.'

Stella paused and looked down. 'Okay then, as you've already got news. Yes, let's walk together, but we'll sit in my car. I can't leave this full trolley for long.'

Rosy sat in Stella's passenger seat, while Stella unloaded her trolley into the boot. She watched in the wing mirror as shoppers walked past and dodged moving cars. Stella's little car was neat and smelled of air freshener.

'All finished,' Stella said, as she got into the driving seat. Rosy was hit by a fear of being kidnapped. As Stella was in the driving seat, she could drive off with Rosy in the car if she became agitated.

Stella said, 'So what did you want to discuss?'

'Did you see my text? I was offering to share the proceeds with you. If we sold it, I mean.'

'And are you prepared to sell it?'

'It's a lovely addition to the tea shop, but if it solves the problem between us, yes I'll do that.'

Stella shot her a look, 'By rights the picture belongs to my family. I am offering to share it with you, if anything.'

'I can see why you're saying that, but it was sold with the building. Don't you want to know how much it's worth? It will probably fetch £4,000 to £5,000 pounds at auction. I was amazed.'

'Mm so my father was right. It was worth something. Although not as much as I'd expected.' Stella finally smiled. 'Oh, go on, I can see you're trying to meet me halfway. Put it into an auction.'

Rosy felt enormous relief even though she could never feel close to Stella again.

'When you set up a tea shop in our bakery, it felt like a steam engine had driven through the village and cleared everything in its path, but I don't hate you,' Stella said.

Looking past Stella's shoulder Rosy noticed a figure heading towards them. 'Is that Jack?'

Stella's eyes widened. 'I don't know. He must be looking for us.'

Rosy felt a lump in her throat, 'I didn't even know that he was back in Sedgeborough. Or. . . perhaps he never left?'

'Difficult,' Stella said. She opened her door. 'I'll head him off.'

She met Jack several metres away. Rosy saw them standing close together with Stella doing most of the talking. She hesitated her hand on the doorhandle, then decided to open the passenger door. She still couldn't hear what was being said. Perhaps Jack was looking for her.

Jack blanched at the sight of Rosy emerging from the car. Rosy smiled grimly. Then she heard a thud as Jack completely disappeared. Rosy gasped.

Stella had dived to kneel on the ground where he was lying. 'Did he hit his head?'

'I think I heard it,' Rosy said.

Stella stroked his cheek. 'Jack speak to me. Are you all right?' She looked around desperately. 'Oh, someone help.'

A man said, 'Shall I radio for an ambulance love? I'll nip to the cab.' He gestured behind him to a taxi.

Jack began to stir. 'What happened?'

'I don't think we're going to need an ambulance,' Rosy spit out, as Stella crooned, 'Are you alright? Can you try to sit up?'

Rosy didn't want to join them. She felt awkward.

The taxi driver looked uncertain but retreated to his cab.

'I'm woozy. I feel sick.' Jack spoke to Stella. He possibly didn't remember that Rosy was there.

'Maybe you should sit here for a while on the tarmac then,' Stella said holding his forearm.

Rosy opened her mouth to speak or even scream, but she clenched her jaw to avoid it. She took a couple of careful steps backwards, then turned and slipped away to her car.

Her thoughts were racing as she threw her shopping onto the passenger seat. Why? Why hadn't she asked them whether there was anything going on? Why hadn't she rushed forward to tend to her ex-fiancé or to find out what he was doing there? As she drove, her hand vibrated on the steering wheel. Eventually she pulled over into a layby. She was shaking. She put the radio on and sat for a moment until she felt ready to carry on driving.

Actually, he was pathetic. He should at least have had the guts to face her. She couldn't see anyone else – her father, Ken, or Hyacinth's husband - acting like that.

CHAPTER 19

Everything in Sedgeborough felt toxic, so Rosy's mood was lifted when she saw the café filled with customers. It was a hectic Saturday, but Mandy greeted her cheerfully. 'Did you have trouble finding them?'

After momentary confusion Rosy remembered, she had originally gone out to get yeast and icing sugar. Her hand flew to her mouth. She dashed back out to the car to collect the shopping. She couldn't concentrate.

'I'm sorry Mandy, can you give me a few moments to collect myself?'

Mandy, superwoman, seemed fine. 'Yeh, don't you worry. I'm well happy keeping busy here.'

Rosy fought away tears. She slumped into a chair in the backroom and took out her mobile. She needed explanations. She scrolled to Jack's name in her contacts. Yes, she would ring him and start the conversation by enquiring after his health. There was no response. He'd blocked her or he'd changed his number. Her jaw ached and her fists clenched. Perhaps she'd go over to the farm and confront Stella.

The door from the tea shop opened. She almost jumped when Ken appeared beside her.

'I'm sorry if I'm disturbing you. Mandy told me to come through. How are you. She said you were on edge.'

'I am.' Rosy let out her breath.

Ken took the armchair beside her and sat quietly. She was glad he had joined her.

'I might lose Mandy soon, you know.'

'If you're referring to their roving lifestyle, it was inevitable. Don't worry we'll manage and no doubt they'll be back.' He paused for a moment. 'Surely that isn't the cause of your present misery?'

She explained what Luke had said, but of course it wasn't the whole story. Ken knew her better than that, but did she want to share her feelings of desolation with him?

'Stella and Jack,' she said eventually.

'Are you saying they're an item?'

'Yes – well no. I'm not saying that, but I've just witnessed them together. He was hurrying across the supermarket car park to see her and then he spotted me. He fainted.' Suddenly she laughed. Ken in turn, smiled broadly. Rosy continued, 'And yes Ken that's what I think. I think they're together. I don't know how to get rid of this feeling. I want to confront them. I need to hear the truth from his own mouth. I hope they weren't together before our wedding.'

'Of course, you're angry. Your own situation with Jack hasn't been resolved. It won't be until the legal side has been dealt with.'

Rosy didn't say anything, but the legal side wasn't the hurtful part of it. Her feelings were raw.

'Come on, Mandy can manage a bit longer,' Ken said, 'I think a walk in the fresh air would help your emotions.'

He did understand. She wouldn't say any more about Jack. She didn't want to load problems onto him, but as they passed the front of the farm Rosy thought of Jack again. Without discussing it, they naturally slowed their pace to check whether Jack might be there.

'This wasn't how I'd planned to take your mind of Jack and Stella. But if your hunch is correct, his car is more likely to be sitting on Stella's drive,' Ken pointed out. 'Perhaps if we go and look at Stella's it will bring you some closure.'

They changed course. Stella's cul-de-sac wasn't far. They didn't need to turn into it to see that Stella's car was in her drive with an unfamiliar Land Rover parked outside beside the curb.

'Well, it might not be his, but he was driving a Land Rover when he came for his stuff. It all fits into place,' Rosy said quietly. Ken stole a glance at her, so she added, 'I know, I sound okay. I'm really not.'

'Come on. Stride out and you'll be able to scream into the wind, high on the hilltop.' They linked arms to stride down a tiny back lane that led to fields. Following a sign for a bridleway, the path led through trees and past a cottage. Rosy realised that they were climbing to a local landmark. There ahead was the stone obelisk that could be seen from the village.

'Is this hill one of the barrows?' Rosy asked.

'It could possibly be. I don't think anyone has investigated it, but the stone obelisk is an eighteenth-century folly.'

After puffing almost all the way up, Rosy stopped to catch her breath. The top of the hill was deserted apart from the sheep that kept the grass well-trimmed. 'This is great. It puts everything in perspective to see all the houses below us looking like a model village. You seem to know the perfect thing for me.'

He turned and studied the view for some minutes. There was still awkwardness since her admission about Ethan.

Ken sighed. 'The countryside always helps. I'd like to go on more outings like this with you as a friend. And for my peace of mind, I need to clear up the issue of Ethan. As you know, I'd had my reservations about him. I found the address of his property business online and then drove over to see it. There was no sign that he was based there, and they hadn't heard of him.'

Rosy was unsettled by the lengths that Ken would go to discredit someone he hardly knew. He seemed so level-headed. Maybe she should be flattered, if his aim was to get Ethan out of her way.

'You weirdo.' She thumped him in the side, 'I suppose he wasn't there because he is here.' She giggled.

'Oh come, he hasn't been in Sedgeborough for that long,' Ken said. 'Someone leaked information to Environmental Health and now to the police about the Animal Rights group. . .'

Rosy had been trying to bat away the threat by being flippant, but she needed to think seriously. 'I sincerely hope that he hasn't leaked anything, I'm already feeling that I'm surrounded by snakes.'

Ken reached for her hand. 'I can see it must feel like that. I promise not to be a snake, and we can build a group of people that are trustworthy. At the risk of you thinking that I'm obsessed, I want to follow Ethan when he goes on one of his weekend absences. Would you like to accompany me?'

Following Ethan seemed to be taking it a bit far, but maybe he was using this as a ruse to engineer time together away from the tea shop. She hoped that would re-establish the easy familiarity that they had always had.

'We'd have to rely on Mandy again, but she seems to be happy to help out. I can see a snag though; Ethan knows my car and he would definitely spot your Rover.'

'Next weekend I'll try to borrow a van from one of the archaeologists,' Ken said.

CHAPTER 20

There were discarded drinks' cartons and sandwich wrappings on the passenger seat. Rosy was grossed out. Ken apologised profusely – he had only just picked up the van.

'Let me brush the seat down for you. Archaeologists, you know what they're like.'

'I didn't. An untidy bunch then.'

'I'm afraid they don't worry too much about appearances. They're always working in mud anyway, so it gets every-where.'

It was still only 8am. Ken wanted to park in the high street within view of Ethan's cul-de-sac, so that they could catch him leaving on one of his regular Sunday trips. He opened some wine gums and offered one to Rosy. She idled away the time scrolling down her phone mes-sages.

'Uh oh, there he goes.' Ken threw the bag of sweets into the glove compartment and started the engine.

They had expected to follow Ethan towards Gloucester, but he was going in the opposite direction. It was excit-ing, just like being in a film, but difficult to stay well back to avoid being noticed. They nearly lost him at a succes-sion of T-junctions. He was heading onto the main Taun-ton road.

'I reckon he's going towards the railway station.' Rosy said suddenly. 'I wonder why, when he already has a car. Maybe it's a long journey.'

Hum,' Ken drummed his fingers on the steering wheel and then waved a 'thank you' to a car that had let them into the traffic queue. 'Or he wants to leave one identity behind when he assumes a new one.'

She was taken aback at his wild imaginings, so she laughed.

When he didn't join in and laugh, she said, 'You really mean that don't you?'

He shrugged his shoulders, hands still at 10 to 2 on the steering wheel. 'Well, it's one explanation. I'll reserve judgement until we know more.'

They were threading through busy streets near the direction of the railway station. There was a risk that they'd lose Ethan in the heavy traffic. They saw him park in the forecourt and walk over to the pay station for a ticket.

Rosy peered around Ken. Ethan was hurrying into the station entrance. 'So now what? We can't follow by car any longer.'

'I think we'd better stay out of the way, but once he's on a platform we could venture in to identify which train he's aiming for.'

'Okay.' Rosy was disappointed but also a little relieved that they were forced to stop trailing their suspect.

It was Sunday quiet. A face was peering out of the ticket

office window at them. There was just one family group of travellers ahead.

She suppressed a giggle and said, 'I'll get in behind them to see what's going on. You stay here. Your height makes you more noticeable.'

One of the younger family members turned to scrutinise her as she tagged along behind their group, but Rosy just smiled. They weren't heading for the same platform as Ethan, but she could see across the railway lines. Ethan had his back to her just two lines over. There was a only broad stairway between them, but she could watch as long as he kept his back to her. She took note of his platform number and then held her breath and kept her fingers crossed while hurrying back. Ethan didn't turn around.

'He's at platform 5,' she announced as she made for the ticket office window. 'Excuse me, which train is the next to arrive at platform five?'

The clerk said, 'That'll be Reading.'

'Okay thank you.'

Ken raised his eyebrows. She sighed as she said, 'I suppose that's that then. We know Ethan goes to Reading.'

'Yes, and he could be changing at Reading, so we don't know much at all,' he said, 'I wonder what our next move is. If we've reached a dead end, we should do something together and enjoy the rest of the day.'

Rosy was pleased. They hesitated as a muffled announcement came over the tannoy. 'I heard Reading,' Rosy said.

'Yes, an apology for delay.'

'Wow there's time to jump on the train without him noticing. How do you fancy a trip to Reading?'

Ken agreed to buy tickets while Rosy nipped to the Ladies. She was bouncing on her heels as she walked back to join him. It was a real adrenaline rush. 'Let's go.'

'No wait,' he said, 'I think we need to hang back until the train pulls in and then get on at the last moment. We don't want Ethan to see us.'

'Yes of course.'

The journey on the train gave them time to chat. Rosy slipped in her question about his previous dating history, but just as she raised the subject they drew up at a small station. They both turned their attention to the window in case Ethan left the train. They didn't see him.

The town disappeared, to be replaced by more views of the rear of houses, cattle in fields, and cars queuing at level crossings. The carriage was stuffy. Rosy guessed the air conditioning was inadequate.

Ken leant his head back against the headrest. 'I'm concerned that Ethan may be a match for us. If he is doing something devious, he will be on his mettle.'

'I don't think he would expect anyone to go as far as to follow him.' Rosy laughed. 'I bet most people would just ask him what he did on Sundays.'

'And how would they know whether he was telling the truth, may I ask?'

Rosy had been mocking Ken's fanaticism, but she felt a twinge of discomfort at his tone. Ken was distant. In fact, he'd closed his eyes as though shutting her out.

'I'm sorry,' she said, 'You've obviously thought it through, and I was trivialising it.'

Ken's eyes sprang open. His warm hand covered her own on the arm of the seat. He grinned. Rosy felt a rush of warmth towards him.

They alighted to the hubbub of Reading station. Passengers were everywhere as they took routes in all directions across the forecourt. Rosy thought, This is it. We lose Ethan now.

They were swept in the crowd towards escalators, but where was Ethan? Suddenly he was ahead of them. They didn't think he'd noticed them, so they made sure that they maintained a safe distance behind. When he left the station, they hung back in the doorway. A woman was waving to get Ethan's attention and when they met, he kissed her. Rosy was sure that she could see child-seats in the back of the car.

She felt like turning away. The kiss left her in no doubt that they were involved. The woman was a little older, slim with long brown hair. She leant in to speak to children in the back and then got into the passenger seat. Rosy felt used. Perhaps it was her own fault and she shouldn't have made the assumption that Ethan was single. It was all twisted in her mind.

'So,' Ken pronounced. 'He says he comes from Gloucester but has a family here. I can't understand why he's keeping his life so secret. It makes people distrust him.'

'Well yes, I must admit we've learned a lot,' Rosy said.

Ken looked into her eyes. 'You look drained. Let's find out the time of the next train to Taunton.'

Rosy closed her eyes, but the station still spun around behind her eyelids.

Ken's voice held a warmth that she hadn't heard before. 'Come on, you sit down while I go and look.' He took her arm and helped her across to a bench, then he disappeared for a few moments, to return with coffee in a tall, disposable cup. He left her with it. Rosy watched the people opposite impassively. Ken's suspicions had been justified. She wondered why Ethan didn't live with his family. He could have just visited Somerset for the occasional day. Perhaps, he was a single dad and the woman just provided childcare. That didn't explain their kiss. Her stomach churned at the conundrum. She took a sip of the coffee. It was surprisingly good considering its packaging.

Ken reappeared full of energy. 'Right. I know which platform we need, and I've bought these,' he indicated glossy magazines under his arm, 'or this Travel Scrabble. Just what the doctor ordered.'

On the train she realised that activity might take her mind off her injured feelings. It was obvious that Ken wanted to play Scrabble and, after initially feeling sluggish, Rosy began to enjoy pitting her wits against him. It had been an inspired idea.

It was dark by the time they left the train to pick up the van in Taunton.

Ken started the engine. 'How does stew and dumplings grab you?' he said suddenly.

'Sounds wonderful. Why? Do you know where we can get some?'

'Well, I set the timer on the slow cooker this morning. I prepared enough for two and it should be ready by now. This is a momentous occasion. A celebration. It will be the first time that I have cooked for you in the cottage.' His voice changed. 'I know you probably don't feel as triumphant about uncovering Ethan's secret as I do, but we can celebrate your Scrabble win. And we'll open a nice wine.' He tucked her hand under his elbow as they walked along. She was comforted.

When Ken opened the cottage door, they were met by a rich aroma. He'd laid a small round table with a white cloth and cutlery for two. He turned on the wall lights.

'You've no idea how welcome this is.' Rosy heaved a sigh. 'It's been quite a day.'

While he was in the kitchen, she had time to examine her feelings. She felt more committed to Ken now, and it wasn't just because both Jack and Ethan had proved themselves untrustworthy. She had spent more time with Ken. Since he'd declared his feelings, she had been contemplating his methodical planning combined with a willingness to go on jaunts like this, his kindness, gentleness and obvious intelligence. She smiled to herself; she had probably been unfair to him.

He produced steaming plates of stew. She might have flirted with him over the meal, but they were both in a quiet, reflective mood.

'I'm glad you came to Sedgeborough,' Rosy said, 'I'm not sure how I'd have been without you here.'

She had needed this respite from her worries. When he removed the empty plates he said, 'Sit down on the sofa and I'll serve coffee.'

Of course, the sofa, she remembered the last time they had kissed there. A lot had happened between them since then and they knew each other much better. He placed the coffee on the table and then concentrated on his phone to select relaxing music. When he joined her, she shuffled closer.

'You can lean on me,' he said, 'both literally and figuratively.'

Rosy felt a warmth creep over her and wanted to melt into his arms. He stroked her neck and inclined his head towards her.

'Rosy. I noticed that you asked about previous relationships. I was married for over ten years.' He stopped and took a sip of coffee and even after that he paused for longer. Rosy wondered whether to fill the gap, but he went on, 'We had the decorators in, and she chose one of the decorators in preference to me. I didn't realise what had happened until she disappeared along with a lot of her possessions.' Ken stopped again and stroked her hair. 'There you have it. It hurt me so badly that I thought I should never recover. That's one of the reasons that I determined on doing this research study. I needed a complete change. The idea of a new relationship has made me very anxious, so you see, when I suggested that we should enter a relationship, I was taking a big risk. But, that's why I empathise with your situation. We've been through the same heartache. It's also why I'm determined that Ethan must not be allowed to hurt you again.'

Rosy felt his hurt. She was pulled towards him like the force of the moon on the tides. Lost in the maleness of his smell, of pipe tobacco and warmth, she felt connected to the beat of his heart. She decided to be bold. 'I think we're much closer. I'm ready to take the step towards a new relationship now. To take the risk as you say.'

He tilted her chin, 'Hmm, a new relationship with me?' his eyes smiled.

Her heart beat faster as she said. 'Yes, I'm ready, but now I realise that it's not so easy for you. Can you take the risk?'

'You are worth it. I've learned about you over the last few months and I don't want to lose you, my darling.'

Rosy was about to comment 'Darling at last instead of dear,' but he interrupted by moving around to face her and placing his lips on hers.

He turned off the wall lights before taking her hand to lead her up the stairs. He barked a laugh, 'I'm sorry I wasn't prepared for this.' He had to remove piles of books from his high Victorian bed and hang his dressing gown up on the door.

'I'm glad that you weren't ready. This wasn't a planned seduction then.' On the bedside table he had a glasses case, an old-fashioned alarm clock and more pipe paraphernalia. It made her smile.

Ken drew the curtains and caught her hand again as he sat on the bed beside her. His kisses were so gentle that they tickled. She put her hand to the back of his neck and looked deeply into his eyes. They weren't aware of time passing. They took it gently, removing clothes one at a time like an unspoken game of strip poker. She was glad to see the intensity in his eyes. It was obvious to her that their love making was more than the physical act.

What seemed like an age later, an owl hooted loudly quite close to the window. 'It sounds as though it's on the roof,' Ken whispered. He sat up to switch on a bedside light before tracing her silhouette with his finger. 'Will anyone miss you?'

'No, my car's still parked at the tea shop.' She looked at his alarm clock. '2.00,' she stretched like a cat. 'I'm relaxed not tired.'

'There's so much more that I want ask you and to share with you,' Ken said. She felt curious about him too. The low murmur of their voices went on until light glowed through the closed curtains. Ken told her that he planned to settle in Sedgeborough. That would be perfect. Rosy felt excited at the possibilities. Only when there was a chirrup followed by a couple more as the dawn chorus began did Rosy fall asleep.

When she awoke, he was propped on one elbow watching her. She loved the smile which spread across his face when she opened her eyes. She had a sudden jolt, 'Oh no, what time is it?'

'Relax, its Sunday.'

'Of course.'

Their dressing was unhurried. They breakfasted on muesli and coffee. Rosy was acutely aware of not wanting to slurp the milk. She spooned muesli daintily, only speeding up when he went into the kitchen for a moment.

'A wonderful day for a dog walk.' Ken looked out of the window. 'We shall have to get a dog. What do you want to do today?'

'I'd love a walk, but I have to put some time in at the tea shop too.'

'Excellent, we'll have a short walk and I'll come and make chocolate eclairs in the kitchen while you do your paperwork.'

CHAPTER 21

Rosy confided, 'I shouldn't even care about the past now. It's all worked out for the best. Thanks to you.' She planted a kiss on his ear. 'But I still want to confront Stella about Jack. She's certainly not welcome in the café anymore.'

'You can't be sure that she split you two up. They might have got together after, but they have kept very quiet about it.'

'What else caused him to change his mind about the wedding? You know what hurts most? She was practically family – she babysat for me and Alex. How old is she for God's sake?'

'You need to consider what your best strategy would be. If you confront her, she will either deny it or escape the situation in some way.'

'You're so good for me Ken.' Rosy sighed heavily. 'Perhaps I should reserve these thoughts for when I'm negotiating with Jack over the Spotted Teapot. I don't know.'

They heard the rumbling of a bus in the distance. 'Oh no, I'm dreading this. That's Mandy and Luke on their way to Wales.'

Mandy and Luke had earned enough to pay for rent on a holiday cottage in the off season. At least they would have a warm winter, she thought. The bus drew to a halt outside.

'We've come to say goodbye,' Luke said.

Rosy poured with tears when she hugged Mandy. 'You were here for me at one of the most turbulent times in my life,' she said.

Mandy murmured in her ear, 'I'll lead us back here next year.' Rosy was thrilled to hear it.

Rosy grasped her by the hands. 'I hope you do. It would be wonderful. We're like a little family.'

'Just hang on.' Mandy dashed back into the bus and returned with a picture grasped in both hands. 'I did this for you.'

Rosy grasped the frame and turned the painting towards her. 'You've painted it? It's beautiful Absolutely fantastic. You did it for me.'

Mandy looked shy, 'I knew you had a problem. It isn't exactly like the other painting of Sedgeborough. It's an updated version.'

Ken said, 'I think it's better.'

Rosy couldn't speak.

Luke flung his arm around Mandy's waist. 'We're glad you like it, aren't we Mand? Will you keep in touch with the group for us? They'll be planning a demonstration about turkeys just before Christmas.'

He turned back to the bus. 'We're going to get a few miles

behind us today.'

Ken and Rosy stood to wave them off. Rosy sniffed away the tears. Ken lifted the picture out of her arms. 'I'll swap the paintings over now for you.'

CHAPTER 22

Ken was spending more time in meetings at the university for the new academic year. Rosy missed him and noticed the gap where Mandy had been too, but she began experiments with Halloween themed cakes for the Spotted Teapot.

She had a new solicitor's letter proposing ways to divide assets, asking her to compensate Jack for giving up his share of the tea shop and suggesting that he share in the proceeds from the sale of fittings. She guessed that this referred to the painting. There was also the suggestion that Jack would stay as business partner while she ran the business day to day.

When she had read it, she dropped the letter onto the table. She would hate to be tied to Jack as a business partner any longer. This new demand about fittings - it wasn't as though the painting was worth millions. She wondered if he wanted to let her know that he was still informed about the business – through Stella.

Everyone had become a potential enemy. This would never do, she took a deep breath and deliberately concentrated on a squirrel bounding across the grass outside. Then grabbed the laptop to make an internet search for possible lenders. It helped her to feel in control again.

She was expecting Ken to come back from Bristol for an evening meal. She decided not to discuss all her worries with him again. He must be getting tired of it. She was going to make a special effort to turn chicken pieces into a Spanish casserole.

Over their meal he asked, 'How was the tea shop?'

She said, 'No tell me about your day. I bet it was much more exciting.'

'Exciting or stressful? These meetings are more about the education business than about archaeology. They want me to be more involved in future planning. I know there are plenty of newcomers itching to climb the ladder. I'm inclined to let them.'

He looked at his plate. Rosy said, 'I can tell that you'd be happier out of there. But can you manage without your university post?'

She didn't want to sound negative so she added, 'I mean, there must be lots of alternatives. As long as you give yourself breathing space to research them.'

Ken put down his cutlery. 'I've been giving a lot of thought to the future. You are right, I don't want to work with the university anymore. You'll be pleased to know that I have enough funds to give me freedom of choice.'

She relaxed. What a wonderful position to be in.

He went on, 'We've been working together in the tea shop for a while. It can be fraught when a couple see too much of each other, but it seems to work for us. I love the process of baking and the atmosphere here.' He smiled. 'Maybe I should say, I love being with you. I wonder whether you would accept a business partnership with me. If I put investment into the tea shop, you could buy out Jack.'

He paused for a comment from her. She had so many responses spinning around her head. He went on to say, 'I wouldn't interfere too much, although I'd like to work here at least part-time. You don't have to decide now. I know it's a big step.'

Rosy didn't need time to decide. She wanted to jump up and down and whoop for joy. Not the most romantic offer, but, whatever, it delighted her. 'That would be fantastic. It would take the weight off my shoulders. I love having you here, Ken.'

He began to eat again. 'You're sure? If you didn't want a partnership, I could just loan you the money.'

'I'm absolutely certain. When your lease runs out, I'd like it even more if you moved in here.' She didn't want to push him too far, but part of her knew that he was ready for that step. Then she felt her own doubt. 'My only worry is that it might have been what broke my relationship with Jack. I want to make sure that it won't do that to us.' She lost momentum. 'How do I do that when I don't really know what went wrong last time.'

Ken reached across to her. 'I'm not Jack. I've had to survive the misery of a failed marriage so I'm not likely to let my pretty little head be turned by Jezebels like Stella. I am sure we will have our challenges. Everyone does, but I know I'd like to live with you.'

She laughed, 'Well that's good to know.' He was right, she

felt completely secure with him.

The conversation seemed over. She was dreaming of a future shared in the tea shop. As they stacked the dishwasher Ken said, 'So, when you get in touch with your solicitor again, will you talk about getting a partnership agreement drawn up.' It was settled.

They channel-hopped. There was nothing on, so they turned again to Scrabble. Halfway through the game they both received texts from Hyacinth. Ken's was a simple invitation to dinner at the farmhouse on Thursday evening. Rosy's said:

'Hi Rosy, I've missed seeing you recently. Would you like to get together for dinner on Thursday evening? I've invited a few others. We need to keep the community spirit going. Luv Hyacinth

We've both been invited. Do you think she has guessed that we're a couple?

She can only know what she's seen, that I am around here quite frequently. I wonder who the other guests will be?

'It would look very odd if she didn't invite Stella and yet surely she'd warn me if she planned to invite Jack.'

Ken said, 'I don't think I'll manage to attend anyway. I am in London all that day at a conference. I suppose I could rush back...'

Rosy had felt close to the family at Manor Farm in the past. It would be a chance to build bridges and it might be easier without Ken there. She would like to plan when they should announce their new partnership, rather than let it slip out. What if Jack were there? It would be just too stressful. She'd turn around and leave again.

There was a high wind with a splatter of rain on the evening of the meal. Rosy was pleased that she'd worn a cosy jumper and trousers. The smell of lamb and rosemary was welcoming when she arrived at the farmhouse. Hyacinth wore a jumper too, although it was a sparkly one.

Hyacinth accompanied her into the room. There was a welcoming log burner in the fireplace. 'No need to introduce anyone, we all know each other. What a pity Ken couldn't come. Stella has cried off too. She's not feeling well. So, it's just you and Ethan, and the family of course. Hyacinth's husband, Brian, and her son stood up. Ethan didn't rise to greet her, but he smiled and patted the seat beside him.

Rosy couldn't forget seeing him in Reading. 'No, it's okay I'll be more comfortable over here on a higher chair.'

Hyacinth moved the dining chair closer to the fireplace, 'Oh dear, Are you not well either?'

'It's nothing, just a twinge in my back.'

Brian led the conversation towards plans for the village bonfire on Guy Fawkes Night. The grandchildren were noisy and excitable but they made Rosy smile. As everyone gathered around the table, Rosy got up to help Hyacinth carry in serving dishes.

She stiffened when she realised that Ethan had been

seated next to her. There seemed no avoiding him. She felt his leg resting against hers as though they were companiable friends. Once the children were whisked off to bed. Hyacinth asked, 'So are you going to stay in the house you're renting, Ethan, or will you buy?'

'I'm not sure of my plans. I'll probably always be coming and going. That's me, I'm afraid. But I feel at home here. That's thanks to you, you've all made me so welcome.' And he made a point of turning to look at Rosy.

Hyacinth turned to Rosy. 'The café's going well? Any more plans for classes? I love the wall hanging I bought from you.'

'No more classes yet. I'm feeling the loss of Mandy.'

'Our eldest granddaughter will be old enough for a Saturday job soon, perhaps she can help out,' Hyacinth said. 'I can tell you, she's not keen on working in the garden centre.'

Rosy nodded. She would see whether the granddaughter followed that up. 'How are the farm businesses developing?'

'Not too bad. We're buying in pumpkins for a pumpkin trail and we have to start ordering early for Christmas in the garden centre of course. We'll have a Santa's grotto this year.'

'Hmm, I can think of a few possible candidates for Santa,' Ethan said, but Hyacinth carried on to say, 'We've no bookings for the Bed and Breakfast and we might not advertise next year. It's a lot of extra work.'

'We're not getting any younger,' Hyacinth's husband Brian said.

'You'd never know it,' Ethan chimed in.

Hyacinth ignored the flattery. 'Well the bed and breakfast ties me to the house. I enjoy being outside and mixing with customers so much more.'

'A good job we haven't got anyone staying at the moment,' Brian added, 'We're watching the flood warnings. It's the highest that it's been. We've worked as volunteers in the past. This looks like it might be a bad one, with high tides and high winds. Of course, our emergency services have flood training.'

Rosy's thoughts went straight to the Spotted Teapot. 'Should I be thinking about sandbags. Where do you get them?'

'We sell them in the garden centre, but I don't think you'll need them – fingers crossed. We're one of the highest villages in the levels. That's why we often help out with flood rescues. We've got a boat at the ready to supplement the Flood Rescue service and sometimes our spare bedrooms have come in handy.'

'A bit of excitement comes to the Levels.' Ethan said. Hyacinth gave him a withering look. He seemed unmoved by it. Rosy began to realise that there was no love lost between them and wondered why Hyacinth had invited him.

Brian suggested a board game, but Rosy felt that this was a good time to leave. She had started to worry about Ken getting back to the village before the roads were affected by flooding.

Ethan said, 'You going now? I'll walk you home.'

'No really, there's no need,' she said, but he threw on his jacket, as she gathered up her bag. There was no stopping him.

Hyacinth, her husband, son and daughter-in-law all crowded into the porch to wave goodbye. Rosy promised to return the invitation. Seeing them all had given her an inner glow despite the weather.

Once they were alone, Ethan said, 'I hoped I'd see you here. We haven't had a catch up since we slept together. I'd been hoping to see more of you.'

'You could have come around to the tea shop anytime. There's no need to ambush me.' She realised that she'd allowed herself to get rattled. 'You can walk along with me, if you like.'

'Looks like I need to. I see you're weaving along the pavement. How much did you drink?'

She lowered her voice; sound carried clearly through the night air. 'No, I'm walking perfectly fine.'

He tried to take her elbow.

At the back of her mind, she wondered if he knew that they had tailed him onto the train. At least he wouldn't dare retaliate here. People would hear her screams and, if she disappeared, Hyacinth would be able to point the finger at him. Rosy gave herself an inner shake.

'Hey I'm sorry. It's time to come clean. My fault.' He held up his open hands. 'I should have got in touch sooner. I really like you Rosy and I think we'd go great together. I'm grabbing this chance to talk because my work's changing, and I'll need to start travelling more. I think our relationship has got real potential and I don't want to lose you.' He raised his voice which rang clear in the night air, 'There, cards on the table. How do you feel now?'

Rosy felt like she'd had a slap in the face - emotions rose in her chest and burst to the surface. 'What do I think? You're a user. Yes you did drop me. You didn't even text. But I had a lucky escape. And I already know you won't be in Sedgeborough, because you're busy in Reading.'

He swallowed hard then dropped his head. He said urgently, 'Listen, I've been looking into groups that may possibly be a threat to Britain's future. I had to be undercover. Its important work.'

'Reading didn't look like work. And there are no groups here that are a threat.'

'Hear me out.'

She shivered at his tone.

'I was assigned to the animal rights groups, so I couldn't be honest with you. They can be a real danger to innocent people.'

She gave a derisory laugh, which hid below it all her hatred of him. 'Oh yes, and what is your next life endangering assignment? An undercover operation checking out the WI's jam.'

Ethan went on quickly, 'I know, the Somerset cell seem harmless – all talk no action. I had to go to my management team to persuade them that there's no further need for undercover work here. They've agreed that I can step down. So now I'm free to be myself with you.'

He stopped under a streetlamp and faced her, then shrugged, 'That's why I've seemed elusive but now I can be yours. There's no woman in Reading.'

Rosy took a step out of his reach before saying, 'I saw you meet her in Reading.'

He gave a twisted grin, 'Perhaps I should be honoured that you took that interest in me. That wasn't my wife.' His face had changed now. She had been right to be nervous. He stepped forward and it felt too close. She couldn't see his face for the shadow of the overhanging hedge. He moved suddenly and she automatically flinched.

He made her skin prickle. She turned and ran. She could hear his steps running after her. She was desperate to get to the 'Spotted Teapot' and lock the door. Then his footsteps died away. He had turned in the other direction and was marching away along the pavement.

Rosy's knees turned to jelly. The Spotted Teapot had never seemed so welcoming. She was disappointed that Ken's car was missing from the drive. She had hoped he would be back from London by now. With shaking hands she put the kettle on and then, despite the hour, she telephoned Tanya.

Tanya's 'Hello,' sounded slurry.

'I'm sorry were you asleep?' Rosy felt guilty.

There was a pause before Tanya whispered, 'Don't worry I was in bed early. I'm awake now and I know you wouldn't phone with no good reason. I'm going to creep into the next room. I've got someone staying.'

'Oh, Tanya it worked out for you. I'm pleased.'

'Yes things are going well. I'd like to come down to see you soon. Once the flooding is over. I heard about it on the news. But what's wrong?' Tanya asked.

Rosy said, 'I've been completely freaked out, but I feel better hearing your voice. I've let myself get terrified of Ethan.'

She was reassured when Tanya told her it was logical to feel terrified in that circumstance. 'At least you know he won't be around so much.' Tanya said. 'You should probably let the others in your group know what he was up to.'

'It's awful. Everyone seems to have a hidden agenda.' Rosy said.

'Except Ken,' said Tanya.

'Yes, except him. Bless him. I don't know where he is. I'm going to wait up for him. He was invited to the dinner tonight, but he couldn't make it – and Stella didn't turn up.'

'Oh no, you're paranoid if you think there's something between Stella and Ken.'

'No of course not. Still thinking of that snake Jack. But why has my old babysitter turned against me?'

Tanya laughed. 'Lust.'

CHAPTER 23

Rosy made a point of listening to the news on the local radio every hour. Schools were all closed, old people's lunch clubs stopped. Very few customers came into the tea shop. She couldn't help worrying about the flood risk. There hadn't even been that much rain, but it had been slow and continuous for days and they were expecting an exceptionally high tide which would be forced up the River Parrett. When they bought the bakery, they were told that it had never been hit by floods, and since then she had read old news reports on flooding. Parts of Langport were often affected but the ordinance survey showed that the road into Sedgeborough was reasonably elevated. There may just be some incursion on the village edge.

Ken was in the garage. There was a lot to sort out now that Luke was gone. Ken would probably use the garage to store some of his belongings once he had given up the lease on his cottage. They only had one customer in the tea shop: a young mother with her toddler.

She lifted her child onto her knee and unloaded an assortment of rattles and soft toys onto the table. She said, 'I needed to get out today. I felt like a prisoner in the house. I'll be glad when we can stop worrying about water, to be honest with you.'

Rosy said, 'I know. But they say Sedgeborough is usually safe. Have you heard anything about the roads into the village?'

The doorbell pinged. Tanya walked in wearing a belted Macintosh and wheeling a large suitcase. It was like a vision.

'Hey, I told you I'd visit,' Tanya said. 'I hope that's okay? Is my old room free?'

'It's more than okay, how wonderful to see you,' Rosy said. She gestured to include her customer 'We were just discussing the flooding. How did you get here? You could have called me for a lift.'

'No need. I drove here myself. I've finally bought myself a car.' Tanya beamed. 'The motorway is absolutely fine, but I was on edge once I got to the backroads. Sometimes I wondered about turning back, especially where the road dipped and I wasn't sure how deep it was going to be. I was able to drive around the worst of it.'

'Rather you than me.' The young mum grimaced.

'I decided to keep going, slow but steady,' Tanya said and sat down at the table opposite her.

Tanya said, 'Hello,' to the little girl in the pushchair, who looked back with an appraising stare.

'Coffees all round, on the house,' Rosy said before sitting down to join them.

Eventually, Tanya went outside to say hello to Ken before going upstairs to unpack. Rosy wanted to know what had really prompted her to arrive so suddenly, but it was difficult to find a private moment to talk.

While Rosy closed for the day, Tanya washed and dressed a salad to go with a lasagne that Ken had made earlier. It was a relief to all get together at the end of the day.

'I'm so pleased you've got a car now,' Rosy said, 'It will make it easy to visit whenever you want.'

'I'm thinking of moving down here actually,' Tanya said. 'I knew I'd need a car for that. I can't imagine living in such a rural area without a car.'

Rosy was intrigued, 'So much must have happened. Do spill the beans.'

'Well, I told you I'd met someone at work. It's going really well. She spends most nights at my flat now. I've told her all about Sedgeborough and well, we've got plans to move down here together. We'll probably rent for a while, but I think we should buy.'

'Hold on, hold on. You've moved so fast. Firstly, I didn't realise your work love was female. That's new!'

Tanya flushed slightly. 'I didn't want to mention it until I was really sure. I have told you that I was bi, haven't I?'

'Maybe you did say something a few years ago.' Rosy nodded. 'So, what's she like then?'

'She's the opposite of me. Totally organised and career driven. That's why I didn't want to cause complications for her at work. She works hard and plays hard. We've been dry-slope skiing and sailing, and we're planning to travel.'

'Wow, that all sounds challenging.' Rosy looked at Tanya

with new eyes.

'Yes, but I'm easily bored. I think Sam's what I've been waiting for.'

Ken said, 'So your new partner is called Sam. We're looking forward to meeting her. I'm moving out of my rented cottage so you could consider there.'

'That's an idea.'

'Why didn't you bring her down?' Rosy said.

'They still don't know at work, so it might have been odd if we disappeared together. I wanted to prepare the ground here too,' Tanya said.

Rosy was disconcerted. 'I hope you knew we'd be supportive.'

Ken had been checking news alerts on his phone and he suddenly looked up with furrowed eyebrows. 'Look, floods have risen all over the levels. It says they're evacuating some villagers into village halls.' He tutted. 'It must be traumatic. Think of the elderly and people with children. I wish we could do something.'

'Hyacinth was talking about previous times. She says that they work as volunteers and have their own boat.

'Mm,' Ken carried on scrolling. 'I wonder who's coordinating the rescue.'

'Let's finish eating anyway.' Rosy gestured to Tanya to hand her the empty dishes.

They had coffee and biscuits without really noticing. Ken decided to phone the council offices even though it was after hours. Extraordinarily, someone answered.

'We've got rescue boats going out. Do you need a rescue?'

'No, Sedgeborough's alright but I was phoning to offer my help.'

'All the boats are out but if you can get to one of the village halls or to the edge of a village, you may be able to join the volunteers that are gathering there. Stay connected. We're coordinating from here.'

As she reached to put the salt cellar back in the cupboard, it slipped out of Rosy's hand. Suddenly there was salt all over the kitchen floor. Rosy felt tears well up. She sat down abruptly.

'We're okay – I know we are. But it's like the world is turning upside down and all I can do is wonder how everyone's coping.'

Ken put an arm around her. His knitted pullover against her cheek was reassuring.

Tanya looked concerned. 'This isn't like you Rosy. You've just dealt with starting a business, what's a little flood.'

The 'Spotted Teapot's' landline rang. Rosy pulled herself together to answer it professionally.

'Hi Rosy, it's Hyacinth here. You've heard about the floods? We're going to take a boat out. We'll look for any people or animals in the outlying areas.'

'Ken's here. He can offer to row.' Ken nodded vigorously. Rosy put the phone on speaker.

'Row! You're a newbie at this Rosy. We're out in the Langport direction now. Can't you hear the roaring. That's the current. No, we've got a motorboat. But if Ken can get down quickly, he'd be a welcome extra pair of hands.'

Ken shouted over, 'On my way.'

Hyacinth added, 'I phoned to ask if you could have the Spotted Teapot at the ready to provide hot drinks.' Without waiting for a reply, she went on, 'And can you run across to the farm. The outer door's unlocked. I've left a huge pile of blankets in the porch. You could bring them to the café to keep people warm once they arrive.'

'Okay,' Rosy's head was spinning.

'Tell her I'm leaving now. Bye.' Ken grabbed his coat and threw a wave in their direction.

'I heard. Thanks Ken,' Hyacinth yelled. Rosy was aware of the background roar now. She glanced outside, the rain was torrential, and the sky was darkening early that day.

'I'll nip to the farm. While you get the tea shop ready for an invasion,' Tanya offered. She hurried into her coat and collected a black bin bag from the kitchen.

Once they had gone, it was as though a typhoon had hit and then spun away. Everywhere felt strangely empty. Rosy's mind shot to Ethan. She hoped he wasn't going to turn up while she was alone. Tanya would be back any minute.

Rosy decided to arrange the furniture around the edge of the room, so that there would be more space for belongings, dogs and wet clothes. She turned the heating up. It would be easiest to provide toast with hot drinks, so she took more bread out of the freezer.

Tanya let in a waft of cold, fresh air when she returned lugging a huge black plastic load.

'I've brought some of them, but there are more in the porch. Do we really need all this?'

'Your guess is as good as mine,' Rosy said. She was itching to get out and see what was going on. She said, 'Can I leave you to look after the tea shop? I think I'll drive down there and find out what's needed. I may be able to ferry some people back in the car.'

The flooding was just the other side of Sedgeborough, so she knew she wouldn't be long.

CHAPTER 24

The heavy clouds made an ordinary twilight much darker. Rosy was glad that she kept a torch in the car. Just where the road dipped going out of Sedgeborough there were figures lit up by floodlights. Rather than get in the way by bringing a car too close, she parked alongside a row of cottages and walked down towards the activity.

Small groups of adults and children were standing, surrounded by bags, dogs on leads, and cat baskets. A professional rescue team, wearing red helmets and with harnesses over their jackets, were moving purposefully. The water was black in contrast to the artificial light. Branches and debris surfed on fast flowing currents. Rosy scanned faces but there was no sign of Ken. Seeing and hearing the speed of water sent her into a cold sweat. She was suddenly fearful of losing him.

A glance back towards the survivors made her feel guilty. She noticed Hyacinth approaching a couple of people who were huddled together for warmth. When Hyacinth spotted Rosy, she waved and drew nearer.

Hyacinth shouted over the roaring water, 'Is the tea shop ready? I think some of these people could come along now. After we've sorted everything out, some of them can stay at the Bed and Breakfast with me.'

'Right, I can take some back with me now. The car's just up there.' Rosy indicated behind her. 'Where're Ken and the others?'

'The men went in the boats. It will take their strength to manoeuvre against the flow and pull people onboard.' Hyacinth had come closer, 'There's a danger from unexpected objects just below the surface but don't worry, the professionals are directing the rescuers.'

With no more time for conversation, Hyacinth was beckoning a middle-aged couple over. 'Rosy here'll sort you out. She'll take you in the car.'

They told her they were Pam and Adrian and they lived a couple of miles away, but they had been caught on the road when a sudden surge of water from an adjoining lane rocked their car. Only their quick thinking in opening the car windows and climbing out onto the roof had saved them. Pam's teeth were chattering. Rosy turned up the car heating. She wondered if Pam was in shock. Their faces relaxed when they saw the lights of the tea shop and Tanya standing in the doorway to meet them.

The coffee machine had never smelt so welcoming. Tanya had put sacking on the floor to soak up water and as soon as they were over the threshold, she wrapped them in blankets and ushered them over to chairs.

More car headlights appeared in the street outside. They could hear car boots and doors slamming before a new influx of people approached. Rosy felt a surge of warmth when she realised that Ken was leading them in. Tanya went into action to greet them all, while Rosy took off her own damp outer clothes. She was surprised when Ken took her elbow and manoeuvred her into the kitchen.

'We've got Stella with us. I wanted to warn you.'

Her heart missed a beat. 'What?'

'We located her on the roof of an outhouse with a chap, I presume it's Jack. It seems they were living in a long, low cottage just outside a tiny village. They had no neighbours to help. I hung onto the gable end to still the craft while they were hauled onboard. She looked sorry for herself when she saw me. Neither of them has looked my way since. What do you want to do?'

Rosy shrugged. 'We can't turn them away. Thank you for telling me.'

Tanya's head flashed in the doorway. She muttered, 'Ah you know about Jack.' She hovered for a moment. 'They've noticed the new picture.'

'Tanya,' Rosy scolded. 'We shouldn't be petty at a time like this.'

Tanya laughed and retreated as quickly as she'd arrived.

There were piles of baggage in the centre of the tea shop. Everywhere there were damp bodies and numerous voices. Rosy's head spun in the next few hours. She tried to ignore thoughts of Jack, but she kept wondering how long he and Stella had been living out there.

She kept herself busy at the toaster. Ken and Tanya acted as hosts. When she peeked at Jack, he seemed thinner in the face and bedraggled. His new life hadn't improved anything then, she thought. Did she still hold feelings for him? She felt revitalised to discover that she didn't. He was a feeble man who had made a mess of everything. Stella sat beside him, but he seemed alone, her focus was on acknowledging villagers and bolstering her reputation.

The hubbub died down when everyone had eaten. Some began to doze.

'I've come to take people over to the B and B. It makes sense to take Jack and Stella with me.' Hyacinth said, 'But Stella has asked, could she have a private word with you first?'

It was tempting to snarl, 'No,' but Rosy wanted some answers and to voice her feelings. She wondered at Stella's cheek.

'Okay, I'll go through into the back room and meet her there. She'd better not bring Jack with her.'

'Um, No, I don't think she'd planned to.'

CHAPTER 25

Rosy was so tense that she paced around the room.

Stella appeared and stood awkwardly. 'I'm sorry Rosy I can see how this looks.'

'Of course, it's clear,' Rosy snapped. 'You and Jack are together. And it looks like you've got a home together near here.'

Stella suddenly sat down. 'That's right, but if I could have saved you from hurt, I would have done.'

'Oh, don't come that. Everything that happened was down to you.'

Stella sighed heavily. 'You could see it that way. I met Jack regularly when I was selling the building to you both. I didn't want to fall for him. It just happened.'

Rosy snorted.

'But I never condoned him leaving it until the wedding to let you down. That was unforgivable, I know he was in turmoil. As a result, he made a terrible job of it.'

Rosy sat opposite her and tried to control her breathing. 'Never mind the idiot out there. You have a responsibility as a friend of my family.'

She noticed silent tears creeping from Stella's eyes. She tried to imagine what was going on in Stella's head. It

155

must have been hard to do the right thing when she was swept up in passion for Jack, but it was still unforgivable.

'I need to know. When did it start? It was before the wedding?' Rosy asked.

Stella hesitated. 'Yes. I'm sorry,' she said quietly.

Rosy felt bile rise in her stomach. 'So you knew what would happen at the wedding.' She clenched and then unclenched her fists. 'I don't think I can forgive either of you, but we have to live in this village. I'm not going to carry on a war against you. I can attack you all I like, but it's that rat out there that did this to me. Ever heard of karma? If I couldn't trust him, you won't be able to either.'

Rosy was even beginning to feel sorry for Stella now. What a turn around. 'Never mind. To be honest, knowing Jack has helped me to recognise how strong and upstanding Ken is. I'm the winner here.'

'I hope you'll remember that when we sort out money. Jack and I want to start some sort of business,' Stella said. Rosy couldn't believe her nerve, but Stella still sat looking contrite. With a sudden movement, she leant over and covered her face. 'I'm so, so sorry. What a mess. I can't imagine what your mum will think of me.'

Rosy stood up, 'Come on.' She gestured to Stella to stand and on a sudden whim she put her arms around her. She was exhausted. 'Let's hope we can all get over this and live our lives.'

As they walked back into the fray it felt, as though something, at least, had been sorted.

Ken cast a worried glance at them as they reappeared. Dear Ken.

'We have beds made up at the bed and breakfast now. If you'd like to move across the street, ladies and gentlemen.' Hyacinth's husband announced.

There was a mass murmur of thank yous. Rosy, standing in the kitchen doorway, watched people go, Jack and Stella among them. Ken called, 'You'll all be welcome to come back anytime. Rosy and I will be running the Spotted Teapot together.'

When Ken made this announcement, Rosy saw Jack spin around with a shocked expression. She smiled.

CHAPTER 26

For the first time ever, they left clearing tables and filling the dishwasher until the next day. Tanya said, 'I'll stay downstairs for a moment. I'm going to phone Sam, and I don't want to disturb you.'

They called goodnight and left her to it. Rosy was more pleased than ever that Ken was staying with her. She fell into bed like a brick falling into sand.

'Every limb aches. It must be stress,' she murmured.

'Mm it has been dramatic tonight,' Ken said. 'I feel strongly about this community now. Now that I've seen my first flooding.'

'First! I'm hoping there won't be anymore,' Rosy said. She felt Ken's warm skin spooning her back and drifted off to sleep.

When she woke the room was bright, although there was still a steady patter of rain against the window. Rosy yawned. She must have been tired; it was 9am already. Ken's side of the bed was empty.

He breezed in. 'Awake at last Sleeping Beauty.' He leant to peck a kiss on her nose.

'Oh yes,' she groaned, 'and there's a lot to clear up today.'

'No Tanya has done that. The decks are cleared for a fresh

start.'

She swung her legs down to the floor.

Ken lowered his voice, 'Don't get up yet. I want to take the opportunity, while we're alone.' He sank onto one knee and produced a ring box. 'Will you honour me by agreeing to be my wife.'

Rosy shrieked. 'What? You pick your moments.' She laughed. 'But of course I will. I thank the day that you came into my life. I would love to be your wife. You make me so happy.'

Ken stood up and pulled her to her feet. Rosy looked down at the open box. A gold ring with a stone the colour of clear blue skies on a cold winter day, nestling on ivory satin.

'It's an antique aquamarine and diamond engagement ring. I've had it altered to fit you. I went to collect it just before the drama of the flood,' Ken said. 'I've been desperately eager to show it to you.'

The aquamarine was a translucent turquoise. She was thrilled by how unique it was.

Ken sounded like a young boy. 'D'you like it? Does it fit?'

She laughed and put it on. 'I love it.'

They were still embracing when Tanya appeared, looking flustered. 'I saw Ken with the ring box. I thought I'd give you two some space. You said yes, of course, but I must see this. Show me?'

'Come in,' Rosy said holding out her finger.

Tanya squealed and hugged her. 'Antique?'

'But of course. It is unique just like Rosy.' Ken smiled.

ACKNOWLEDGEMENT

With thanks to members of the Leakey Pens writers' group who provided valuable feedback on my work-in-progress: Sandra, Paul and Joy. Not forgetting Mo for your encouragement and advice on flooding.

PRAISE FOR AUTHOR

From a review of the Boatman's Daughter, first book of the Retro trilogy.
"Excellent descriptions of the 1970s period highlight how different life was even such a short time ago, from furniture and food to technology and social attitudes. The characters are so well drawn they feel like friends. A good light read to entertain and surprise."

- JANE MOON

A second review of the Boatman's Daughter.
" I think the book captures the vibe of the seventies, reflecting the choices and attitudes of the time. Look forward to more

from this author."

A review of Echo of the Past.
"Well done on writing an entertaining story about a sensitive and often hidden topic."

- *ADVANTAGE SOCIAL ENTERPRISE CIC*

BOOKS BY THIS

AUTHOR

Retro

A trilogy which stretches from the life of Imogen, a girl in the early 1970s, her mother, Ceci, establishing life in a commune in France, to the the 1990s, when, Diana, discovers more about her family's past.
(These three books are also available as separate ebooks)

Echo Of The Past

A prequel to the Retro trilogy. In the 1960s, Maura comes from an Irish Catholic background, is growing up in London. We see what happens when she gets to know an American with Irish ancestry.

Printed in Great Britain
by Amazon

11431848R00099